AS IT IS ON

TELLY

BY

JILL MARSHALL

ABOUT THE AUTHOR

Jill Marshall is the author of many best-selling books for children and young adults, as well as adult fiction including The Most Beautiful Man in the World.

She's most well-known for her series about sensational girl spylet, Jane Blonde which has been a best-seller around the world.

She lives in leafy England and does some globe-trotting, when not writing, writing about writing and talking about writing.

Jill's books are available in several formats. Go to www.jillmarshallwriting.com for more information.

CHAPTER ONE

Bunty realised that her marriage was probably over, once and for all, the day she received the bill for her husband's vasectomy.

She threw the offending envelope across the breakfast table. 'What the hell's this?'

Graham scanned the letter, a liverish flush seeping up his neck. 'Bollocks. It's an invoice. I told the woman I didn't need an invoice.'

Bunty shook her head in disbelief. Trust Graham to answer the wrong question. 'What the hell's this' hadn't actually referred to the piece of paper, the printed statement of the fact that her husband had, unbeknown to her, checked himself into hospital and paid someone several hundred pounds to sever the tubes to his future paternity. His answer was not 'Oh, maybe I should have told you about that,' or 'Ah, yes, well the doctor said I had to for my particularly horrible and life-threatening medical condition and I didn't want to worry you,' or even 'Bloody hell, that's some amazing mistake – as if I'd have a vasectomy without you knowing!' No. He was only annoyed because they'd billed him at home.

Graham's *non* sequitur was supreme evidence of their growing distance from each other. Alienation. He was actually starting to look a bit like an alien, thought Bunty. Green-tinged. Ears sticking out even more as the hair on his pate thinned. A strand of Orange Shred stuck in his teeth. No, not an alien, she realised. Shrek. Her husband looked like Shrek. Perhaps it was a very good thing that they wouldn't be having any more children. Even so, she would have liked it to be a joint decision. Something they'd discussed. Even mentioning it in passing in a cast-off 'Don't forget the dry cleaning,' manner would have been an improvement.

'So,' she said slowly, making sure that Graham could fully comprehend what her point was, 'you went off to have a vasectomy, didn't tell me or even ask me what I thought, and then put the bill on my Visa card. What is wrong with this picture?'

'Don't you go getting all holier than thou. I do pay for the bloody card,' said Graham, not unreasonably, as he did, indeed, foot the bill for all of Bunty's expenditures on credit. They weren't exactly excessive, however, and she couldn't quite follow Graham's logic when he added, 'And you put all your haircuts on it. Once a month, a hundred quid, it all adds up.'

Bunty drew herself up to her full four feet eleven-and-a-half inches. 'Graham, it's not really the same thing, is it? I go to the hairdressers once a month because my hair, you know, grows back. Your chopped tubes won't grow back. Sperm won't start popping out of your hair follicles. You've just taken this unilateral decision that affects our whole future, and didn't even tell me. Were you ever going to tell me? Has this bill just ballsed up the whole 'keep Mrs Graham in the dark' plan? No pun intended.'

At this, Graham had the grace to look a little shame-faced. The dull maroon mottling his cheeks flared a little. 'It's not as if we've not talked about it though, Bun. You've said yourself you couldn't stand another child, another one like Charlotte; how you've had to devote your whole life to this ungrateful human who treats you like a bank-slash-hotel-slash-chauffeur ...'

That was, in fact, true. She had said all those things. Sometimes she'd even meant them. Much as Bunty loved her newly teenaged daughter, the thought of having *two* morose, monosyllabic Pod People (or should that be iPod people) slamming doors and bumping into furniture did not fill her with any desire to frog-march Graham into the bedroom and procreate. Come to think of it, though, there wasn't a great deal that could persuade her to get Graham into the bedroom these days. Several pints of rough chardonnay combined with a heady dose of sunstroke had been the cause last time, and with the slight scare over the day-late period heightening to full-on hysteria, Bunty could see why Graham would assume she didn't want any more kids.

She could almost have felt sorry for him – if she'd actually believed him.

'You said it was a squash injury,' she said accusingly, pushing her toast away from her in disgust as she remembered him staggering around the bed trying to get into his trousers, wincing, cradling his blackened scrotum like a newborn kitten.

Graham smiled weakly. 'It was, sort of. Squashed tubes.'

'Funny.'

What the hell's happened to us, she thought. Bunty propped her head on her hand, with its chewed fingernails and wilting plaster from yesterday's contretemps with the tofu she was chopping for Charlotte's new vegan diet, and stared at her husband. He'd always been dependable, solid. That's what she'd loved about him. So unlike her other flighty boyfriends. He was the one with the sensible job in insurance, the Volvo instead of the Ford Capri, the two-pints-after-rugby-then-straight-home mentality. Getting a surreptitious vasectomy was by far the most spontaneous thing he'd ever done. Or maybe it wasn't spontaneous – perhaps he'd been planning it for years, sneaking off for consultations with the gonad doctor. Maybe it was a woman. He'd been having an affair with the gonad doctor, and couldn't justify any more visits without actually getting the chop. To foil the receptionist, he'd allowed his manhood to be physically attacked. She could picture the whole scene, à la *General Hospital*:

Graham: She's onto me, I'm sure of it.

Sexy Gonad Doctor: (hoisting Graham's legs into callipers) But how could she know?

Graham: Perhaps three visits a week was a bit excessive.

Sexy Gonad Doctor: (removing her surgical mask) Then kiss me. We may not be able to do this again.

Scene ends on Graham, legs waving like a dying insect, being leapt on and straddled by Sexy Gonad Doctor, her lips puckered.

It was rather difficult to imagine though, even for Bunty and her over stimulated creative bent, now that his dependability had morphed into potato-on-the-couch dimensions. It was hard to get him interested in anything other than the football results and the occasional afternoon visiting the local steam railway, where Bunty became infuriated at the way he turned all *Thomas the*

4

Tank Engine, droning on about the grand age of steam as if he'd been born in the Victorian age, in the home counties, instead of in Sheffield in the sixties. He was still solid all right, too solid in certain parts – his stomach, for instance, which had very nearly blocked his view of the offending groin; and the lardy parts where his shoulder blades used to be. Although … Bunty peered more closely across the marmalade jar. Hadn't he lost a chin? And he had been going out rather more recently. Squash, he'd said. Right. Maybe his tubes weren't the only things he was having chopped off.

Graham stared back at her for a few moments, then slurped back the rest of his coffee, apparently satisfied that Bunty would not be giving him the third degree. Time to make his escape. He motioned towards the lounge, where his briefcase was resting on the sofa, ready to be picked up, along with his laptop, mobile phone, mobile phone charger, and diary with newly tested ballpoint pen. ('I always write my appointments in my diary. Love this technology, but wouldn't totally trust it.'). He looked longingly at the couch. 'I'd better …'

Better what? Shag the babysitter on the sofa? Kristiana was twenty-six and on the buxom side; Charlotte didn't really need a babysitter so much as a jailer these days. Or perhaps he needed to delve behind the cushions and find some more bills. For handcuffs. A Porsche. Plastic surgery (what had happened to that chin, after all?) Quite clearly, Graham was going through the mid-life crisis to end all mid-life crises. If he actually had a secretary he'd no doubt have cast off Bunty and announced the engagement by now – a new blonde model, barely older than

Charlotte, not care-worn and slightly shrewish about it, as Bunty knew she had become, and flexing the credit card with her outrageous need for monthly haircuts to hang onto her gamin looks.

With a sigh, Bunty watched Graham's retreating back, looking for evidence of love handles and finding that they, too, had dwindled distinctly. She got to her feet and started clearing the table. 'Take Charlotte to the bus stop, will you, lo— Graham?'

Graham stopped adjusting his cufflink, taking in the dropped 'love,' then nodded briefly. 'Charlotte! Going now,' he yelled up the stairs.

Their daughter appeared, iPod wires trailing from her ears as if she'd just unhooked herself from a battery charger (and there were times she could certainly do with it). She jammed her hat down over the fresh cluster of spots along her hairline, dropped her skirt two inches further down her hips so that the hem tickled her ankles and a line of pale lumpy flesh appeared above the waistline, and scuffed her way over to the kitchen bench.

'Morning, darling,' called Bunty cheerfully.

Charlotte raised an eyebrow. 'I hope you've not made that heinous disgusting tofu mush you made yesterday,' she pronounced, stuffing her sandwich box into her backpack. 'There were red bits on it, like blood or something, and it was totally gross. I'm a vegan, Mother, I can't eat stuff with blood on it.'

'It was blood. Mine,' said Bunty cheerfully. 'And don't call me Mother.'

Charlotte paled even more, sticking her tongue out like some pubescent gargoyle. 'That is foul! How could you give me food with actual blood on it? Forget the lunch, I'll get something myself. Dad, you got a tenner?' Being vegan didn't mean checking on the animal fat content of the local chip fryer, apparently. Bunty offered her cheek up for a kiss, and after much rolling of the eyes, Charlotte obliged. 'Later, *Mother*.'

'Love you too,' said Bunty.

She favoured Graham with a look that she hoped said, 'Approach if you dare,' and watched them leave, standing with folded arms at the lounge-cum-diner-cum-kitchen window. Waiting. Waiting for some emotion to swamp her once they'd left the house, vacated her territory, allowed her to become Bunty, Person, once more.

Nothing.

As she pushed the trolley around the supermarket an hour later, having loaded the dishwasher, arranged for someone to come and check the drainage in the back garden, and given the floor a desultory flash-over with the vacuum cleaner, Bunty worried that there was something missing. Not from her life. From her. In the last couple of hours she had discovered that her husband, who she'd always considered too docile to be bothered to have an affair, was gearing up for a shag fest. Knowing how reluctant Bunty had been to partake in such events in the last few – what was it? Weeks? Months? Almost into years, now she thought about it – then she could hardly imagine the shag festee was meant to be her. Graham was losing weight, sneaking out for furtive ball-gropings, albeit by legitimate ball-gropers perhaps, and having the route to financial claims by aggrieved new mothers firmly and surely cut off. And yet she still felt nothing. Nothing more than perhaps a mild curiosity as to when he'd been planning on leaving her. Or perhaps he wasn't planning on leaving her. He could be standing in the adulterer's patisserie, rubbing his fat paws together at the prospect of the cakes he could have, eat, or just lick from time to time. Surely that should instil some sort of emotion in her?

She paused over the fresh figs, immediately reminded of the spectacle of Graham's engorged gonads, and to her immense surprise and the alarm of the nearby pensioner choosing potatoes, she laughed out loud. It still didn't seem feasible. If anyone was going to have an affair, she had always assumed (as had Graham, thus far) that she would be the adulterer. Bunty the flirt. Bunty the tease. Bunty the tamed wild-child. In fact, it had been far too easy to provoke Graham into a state of mouth-frothing jealousy with just a few more smiles than were strictly necessary, the touch of a colleague's arm. At first she had thought it sweet, how easily she could goad him into a frenzy. Recently, she'd treated it more like sport. Something to alleviate the boredom.

Suddenly she realised why she wasn't actually *feeling* anything about Graham's debauchery and wild dissembling. She was bored. Bored catatonic with her ordinary life, her ordinary house, her ordinary, ordinary family – now so very ordinary that her husband had hit forty just ahead of her and was moving on. This wasn't how it was meant to be. She'd been the girlfriend of rising rock-stars. Like Adam, who would have been great in

Take That but was too pretty for the ZZ Top of Taunton he'd played for. Too pretty for her, in the end, or the many other bimbos he'd bedded over the months of their relationship. Nevertheless, she'd been the one he'd cried over, written songs for, begged for forgiveness. How could she have traded all that, and the dancing on tables and the vodka-induced skinny-dipping on the Taunton shore, for this? For Graham? For ... Ordinary?

It wasn't until she reached the checkout that that she remembered that Graham's big attraction had been his healthy bank account. Heaving steak, half a dozen bottles of wine and a whole camembert for baking in its wooden box smeared in honey like some fifteen-year-old wonder chef on the Food Channel had done, Bunty packed up her bags, swiped her loyalty card and handed over the Visa before the lady behind the till had even spoken.

'Sorry, how much?'

The operator, sporting a very dubious auburn rinse, grinned cheerfully. 'Miles away, were you, love? Happens all the time. One hundred and twenty-three pounds and forty-five pence.'

'Oh Christ!'

It was no more than usual. Too much, but no more than usual. But the feeling in her gullet was far from the norm. Handing over her credit card, she heard Graham's voice in her head, telling her that he paid the credit card bills. He did. And the mortgage, and Charlotte's exorbitant private school fees that would have funded a whole state school for a year, and the frequent haircuts.

That was why she had settled for Graham. For dull, steady Graham. He was her very own Flexible Friend. Adam had squandered more than just her love. His requests for money had become more and more frequent. Not until years later, when she was investigating the whole issue as a means of making sure Charlotte avoided it, did she realise that the amounts and frequency of the loans had been directly related to the redness of his eyeballs, the terrible sniffing, and the sallow waxen finish to his skin. Most of the trust fund her great aunt had left her to help her in her education, to set her on her own feet in life, had gone up Adam's nose.

And then there'd along came Graham, her financial advisor, helping her to save what she hadn't already wasted on her un-ordinary rock-star hopeful of a boyfriend. He had given her low risk options, locked the last remaining couple of grand into a long-term account that she couldn't get to, and moved her into his own house within ten days. The fact that a man in his early twenties had a house at all had not struck her as odd; he was her hero, her saviour, and her anti-Adam.

So that's how it had been for the last sixteen years. Mr Dependable and Grateful, shocked out of his usual steadiness by his adoration of this Bambi, this fawn of a girl, and Ms 'I settled'. Bunty didn't like thinking that she'd gone for any easy option, but deep down she suspected that if Graham had been less free with the bill-paying, she might have been a bit less free with her love. Of course, she wasn't that shallow. They'd got along, very well on occasions. When they weren't getting along very well, they were getting by. Just fine. And she did love him. How could she not? But did she still? Had she ever ... really?

'Pin number, love?' the cashier was saying.

'Sorry. Sorry.' Bunty keyed in her code, fighting the temptation to hyperventilate.

There was the crux of it. She'd believed he would never leave her. But now he was doing the unthinkable. And no Graham meant no bill paying. No hairdressing. No steak and wine and whole hunks of imported cheese. It would be no fun whatsoever. And she had no discernible talent, other than flirting, with which to make a living for herself.

She stared wildly at her bottle of Penhaligon wine, vastly overpriced because of the import duty from New Zealand. It would all have to stop. Graham wouldn't see her penniless, she was sure, but the blonde bitch he was likely to take up with would overtake her in the hairdressing stakes, demanding fortnightly highlights. They'd have children. Charlotte would be tossed aside and sent to the local comprehensive, running the gauntlet of the drug runners and knife gangs that Bunty was convinced populated the whole place.

At last her whole chest cavity was flooded with emotion. It wasn't what she'd imagined – grief, sorrow, sadness for the loss of her husband. It was fear – pure white, flashing, asphyxiating fear. She was about to be discarded from their marriage and she had no options.

'I need a back-up plan,' she informed the cashier hoarsely.

Mrs Auburn frowned. 'Is that like the loyalty card? You'll have to go to customer services.'

'Customer services.' Bunty nodded rapidly, sweeping carrier bags off the conveyor belt and into the shopping trolley, oblivious to the crash of glass, the drip of prized NZ sauvignon blanc onto the tiles.

Back-up plan. Back-up plan. That was it. She chanted it like a mantra as she jogged to the car. It wasn't customer services she needed. It was Kat.

CHAPTER TWO

Kat listened without comment to Bunty's plan, as Bunty had known she would, particularly when confronted with a nibble platter of Sainsbury's best and a large glass of what she had managed to salvage from the shattered wine collection.

As Bunty drew to a close, Kat nodded, put her glass down, and said, 'You're kidding, right?' in a tone that suggested she knew full well Bunty was entirely serious. Bunty gazed levelly at her, fixing Kat's wide blue eyes with her own almond-shaped hazel ones. Unblinking, Kat stared back at her. She wasn't really waiting for an answer, although she was hoping for one. Kat knew Bunty far too well for that. They had been friends since their early twenties, when Kat had worked briefly for the same company as Graham, and they had both run rings around him. She had the kind of sweet nature that would have made her a far more suitable partner for the trusty Graham, but at that time she had been focussing on her career. Unfortunately, that now meant that she was heading into her late thirties without a partner, desperate for children and contemplating the turkey baster. Matters had improved lately when she started a relationship with Simon Francis, but since he lived on the other side of the world, babies seemed somewhat off the agenda.

'Go on then,' said Kat eventually, topping up both their glasses. 'How exactly do you think you're going to manage Operation Sugar Daddy? Mmm, like the sound of that. I should get one,' she added, far more keen on the 'sugar' element than the 'daddy' part.

Operation Sugar Daddy. Bunty liked the sound of it too. She had worked it out in the car as she bounced the Mini off several kerbstones, driving home from the supermarket with the mobile attached illegally to her ear and her heart in spasms. It made sense. What was going to happen to her? Graham would trade her in for his newer model, and she would be cast aside like the weekend's papers. What could she do about it? Very little, assuming that the vasectomy, weight loss and subterfuge over the squash games meant what most wives would try to ignore – that Graham was already test-driving someone new. So how was she going to live?

That was the critical question. There would be alimony, of course, and Charlotte's upbringing paid for. The courts would see to that. She'd probably get the house if she pushed hard enough, although for some reason, the prospect of downgrading rather appealed. A cosy terrace in Brighton, maybe. Close enough to commute, far enough away to start again. Less rooms to clean; less bland magnolia and beige tiles (beautiful, expensive, but still beige) in the double shower, which had never been used for more than one person – at least to her knowledge.

But what could she actually do? She had no skills, no trade, no experience, not even any ancient qualifications. Breaking up with Adam had caused her such grief that she'd given up on her A levels, done odd jobs, and lived off her aunt's legacy until Graham had stepped in and taken charge. Having spent the fifteen years trying out coffee groups, testing pottery classes, tennis and various other hobbies to fill in time while Charlotte was at school, and becoming the world's leading expert on daytime TV, she had nothing to offer any employer. Nada. Nil. The only advantages she had that she could possibly utilise were her naturally skinny frame and long-lashed eyes that could be batted at opportune moments.

Previously that had been purely for sport, to wind Graham up. Now she had to put those traits to good use. If Graham could trade up to someone newer, shinier, then she too could upgrade. To someone fun. Someone sexy. Someone … she hated to think it would come to this, but the truth was staring her in the face … someone rich. As Graham had pointed out after the Adam debacle, it was just as easy to fall in love with someone wealthy as it was with someone impoverished.

Bunty took a slug of her wine. 'I don't know how to do it. That's why I need your help. I don't even know where to start. You did all that dating stuff, didn't you?'

'Me?' Kat belched out a hollow laugh. 'Yes, you see how successful it was for me. I couldn't find anyone for myself. Had to have Cally's cast-offs.'

'Well, there's a thought. Cally's cast-offs,' said Bunty with a grin. 'You and me. The Cally's Cast-offs club.'

'Don't even think about it.'

Cally, the third member of their trio, the three musketeers, had gone from closeted single-motherhood with daughter Paige to unmarried bliss with her sort-of father-in-law, via a near miss with his son, her ex, Alan, and with the delicious Simon Francis. Kat now had her talons into Simon, though admittedly at rather

15

a distance. And Alan … Well, Bunty didn't want to think about that too much. It had been revealed on the eve of Cally's wedding to Alan that Bunty and the groom had once snogged at a party when Alan was already involved with Cally and Bunty, to her shame, was married with a young baby. It had only been a kiss – a sad, desperate, clinging-to-a-life-raft type of a kiss that had led to nothing. Bunty had cringed about it throughout her marriage. Infidelity did not come naturally to her. And yet Graham seemed to have taken to it with ease. In fact, with considerable skill and forethought, the vasectomy enabling him to have sex with impunity.

'Oh my God,' she blurted, squirting wine through her teeth. 'I just thought of something. You know last year when we were in Fiji for Cally's wedding – nearly wedding? Do you think it started then? I bet Graham started shagging around as soon as my suitcase was in the taxi.'

Kat cocked her head sympathetically. 'You had just left him, Bun-Bun. He might have even … had a right?'

'It was a trial separation. One month. And … oh, bloody hell, he's got a nerve.' More memories flooded back to her. Graham looking all persecuted and wounded when one of their many arguments had led to her confession of the Alan-snog. It had been meant to reassure him, let him know that that was the very worst she'd ever done; instead, he had informed her their marriage was over and she ought to move out. 'He was *looking* for an excuse. He actually wanted a little holiday from our marriage. Think about it – he had the perfect excuse for heading off to look for someone else. He was hurt. I'd cheated on him. I'd left him. He was rethinking our future.'

'Exactly the time he'd start an affair with someone. A sympathetic work colleague. Someone who 'understood him'.' Kat was away, thoroughly enjoying the *Cosmo* psychobabble. 'Just one drink too many and one thing leads to another. It's actually quite romantic.' She caught Bunty's eye and swallowed hastily. 'Sorry. I'm sure none of that happened. He took you back, didn't he?'

He had taken her back. That much Bunty had to concede. She'd come back from Fiji, chastened by the exposure of her past tiny indiscretion and the near loss of her cherished friendship with Cally, bewildered by the fact that she could ever have been attracted to Alan in the first place – such an Adam-type – and begged Graham to try again. 'It was only because he had such a hard time with Charlotte,' she said. 'He had no idea what it was really like to deal with a truculent nearly twelve-year-old, day-in day-out.'

Charlotte had started her periods while Bunty had been away, and Graham's handling of the situation had been of the chocolate teapot variety. Both Charlotte and Graham had fallen on her with cries of delight when she'd returned from Fiji with an olive tan and collection of raffia ornaments. Mum was home. That was what they'd both thought, she was sure. Mum was home. Not Bunty. Not Graham's wife. Just someone who could deal with hormones, menstruation and homework logs.

Bunty's eyes filled up and she almost rejoiced. At last – some sort of regret! 'I can't believe I was so taken in,' she said softly, waggling her empty glass at Kat. 'Of course he'd need me here. He couldn't go off to all those, ahem, squash games with Charlotte hanging around his neck, could he? It's probably been going on all this time.'

'I'm afraid you're probably right,' said Kat. 'The signs are all there.'

'So what do I do?'

Kat smiled, patted Bunty's hand and sauntered over to the computer. 'Operation Shug D begins. That's code, so Graham doesn't know what you're up to and chuck you out first.'

With a few agile taps of the keyboard, she brought up Match.com. Page after page of photographs panned across Bunty's eyes. 'They all look like convicts,' she said. 'I can't meet any of them. I might never get home to Charlotte. They might actually be *after* Charlotte.'

'They're not that bad, really. Most of them take their own photograph, and it always looks terrible, like they're looking in a hub-cab, or the back of a spoon. But the ones you want to be careful of are the ones with professional photos. Usually idiots. Big egos.'

Bunty drew in a deep breath. 'I don't care about the size of their egos. Just their wallets. How about that one?'

She pointed to an Onassis-looking chap half-silhouetted against a soft background, billowing chins flowing down his chest like the ruffles on a dress shirt.

'Eeuw,' said Kat. 'You are not that desperate.'

'Not yet,' said Bunty darkly. She drained her glass.

But after a hysterical half-hour trawling through the pages, Bunty had to agree that she really was not that desperate. It was fine to imagine that all she was really interested in was income, but when it came down to it, it simply wasn't true. The ones who specified that their income was substantial tended to sound like arrogant pricks; the ones who looked good appeared either to be car mechanics (and not the garage owner) or police officers with 'very open minds, looking for fun'.

'This is hopeless,' she said, after 'ROByoublind' had outlined his spiritual journey on his yacht and included details of his many experiences of Tantric sex. 'They all sound like pervs, or no-hopers. I can't go meeting them all in the hope of finding one who's looking for a … well, a wife.'

It was all she knew how to be, and yet most of the characters on the screen seemed to be searching for fun, or friendship, or possibly relationship after friendship ('they're the ones that are just shagging anything that moves,' Kat had told her knowledgeably).

Kat looked up thoughtfully. 'You're absolutely right. You're after something quite specific. Someone looking for marriage, with a good income. Let's say … six figures as a minimum?'

'Sounds good.'

'Well, they might be there on these ordinary sites,' said Kat, pulling the keyboard towards her, 'but I'm betting they go somewhere more exclusive. Why don't we look up … um … 'wealthy males searching for love'.'

Bunty shrugged. 'Are they really going to be listed on here? I did see something like that on *Doctor Phil* once – 'Millionaire

Marriages' or something. But that was in America, Hollywood even. There won't be anything like that here.'

'Google will find them.' Kat smiled mysteriously and started to type in 'wealthy' with a flourish.

Before she'd got as far as the 'e', a drop-down menu appeared before their eyes, and the images of hopeful Matchdotcommers shimmied out of the way for some new pictures.

'Oh my good God!' screamed Bunty. 'Turn it off. Off!'

Kat fumbled with the mouse. 'I didn't … How did that …?'

'Christ, if Charlotte ever saw that lot …'

They watched, horrified, fascinated, as the noughts-and-crosses board filled with images of a variety of penises faded away, along with the photo of Prince William (his face, not his penis) and, inexplicably, a bearded older man who apparently was writer and comedian Willy Rushton.

'How the hell did they come up? What's that got to do with 'wealthy'?'

Kat peeked through her fingers at the screen. 'Are they gone? How disgusting. I don't know how they got there. I'd only typed in "w" …' She peered more closely at the screen. 'Oops!'

'What?' Bunty thrust her head over her friend's shoulder. 'What does 'oops' mean?'

Kat pointed to the drop-down menu that had appeared with the insertion of the letter 'w'. Every item beginning with that letter that had been searched for over the last few months was listed there. Wealth management – that was probably Graham. Wicker chairs – Bunty, looking to replace the ancient Lloyd Loom in their bedroom. And top of the list: willies.

Bunty felt sick. 'Jesus. Was that Charlotte?'

'I'm guessing … yes.' Kat grimaced, then tried not to giggle. 'What else has she been looking at?'

They spent the next fifteen minutes thinking up rude words that might have been keyed in by a thirteen-year-old girl and her friends, striking out with most but hitting gold with 'people having sex', 'viginas' (which, amazingly, had over four hundred entries despite the misspelling) and the one that finally floored them under the listing for 'b'– big wiggling bums.

Bunty smacked Kat in the side. 'It's not funny.'

'Big wiggling bums? It's hilarious.' Kat's cheeks were pink with constrained giggles.

Bunty's face broke too. 'Maybe she meant 'Buns'? Something to do with me?'

'Since when did your arse look like that?' shrieked Kat, unable to hold it in any longer.

They held onto each other, sobbing with laughter, until a horrible thought occurred to Bunty. 'Kat, what if they're not all Charlotte? I mean, I can see the willies and what have you being her doing, but 'big wiggling bums'? Like you said, my arse has never looked like that.'

At which point, Kat looked rather green. 'Oh. Sick bastard. Most men would be overjoyed with your pert little tush. They certainly prefer it to my chair-wobbler.'

The picture of the woman Graham was involved with was becoming ever more clear. It might even, she thought with horror, be pictorially clear to Charlotte. Getting Netnurse, or whatever it was that stopped children looking up 'willies', might not be enough. Not nearly enough.

Bunty swallowed back bile and reached past Kat to the keyboard. 'Millionaires looking for love' she typed.

At the top of the list was the Croesus Club.

'Are you sure you're ready?' Kat's fingers hovered over the enter button as she stared anxiously at her friend.

Bunty nodded across the keyboard. 'Hit it,' she said.

To: admin@croesusclub.com
From: bunty123@ntsworld.com
Profile:
Club Name: Sugar Bun
Sex: F
Age: 35
Income: n/a
Appearance: I've been told I look like Audrey (Hepburn or Tatou, take your choice). Photo attached. Obviously I'm older than one of them and younger than the other one (or, at least, still alive).

Seeking: I am a traditional lady who likes to be at home seeing to the domestic affairs (and that does not mean AFFAIRS) of my busy, professional husband. Seeking a kind, handsome, athletic man who appreciates that in a woman. Non-smoker preferred. I love art galleries and museums, fine wines, and fencing. Please, please, please – utter discretion. My husband doesn't know I'm doing this.

Payment by: VISA. It's being used for all sorts these days.

From: admin@croesusclub.com
To: buntymckenna@ntsworld.com
Thank you for your query and payment for membership of the Croesus Club, where the wealthy can also find love.

I'm afraid we have very strict membership rules, and one of those is that our members be single. Of course, we apply the strictest discretion at all times, but we cannot accept you as a member if you are, in fact, married.

Perhaps you could confirm this point for us before we investigate your membership further.

Kind regards

Priscilla.

To: admin@croesusclub.com

From: buntymckenna@ntsworld.com

Dear Priscilla,

Oops. That was meant to be a joke! Of course I'm not married. As if I'd be looking for a new husband while I still have the old one. I was trying to display my GSOH, but obviously that fell a bit flat. My SOH is temporarily AWOL. Many, many apologies, and I hope that you can look into my membership again.

Yours very sheepishly

Bunty

To: buntymckenna@ntsworld.com

From: admin@croesusclub.com

Of course. We have deducted four hundred pounds from your credit card, and look forward to a long and happy relationship – ours, and yours. Our consultant will call in the next couple of days with details of your first rendezvous.

Best wishes

Priscilla

CHAPTER THREE

For the next couple of days, Bunty skulked around like someone with a body buried in the garden. Even her dreams ran along the same lines: she crept around corners, avoiding the police, knowing that somewhere, recently, she had inadvertently killed someone and stowed them under the patio. Graham, smirking, would hint that he knew, that he was calling in forensics, that she would suffer endlessly for what she had done ... *CSI* had nothing on him. Having had quite a lot of time on her hands to look into these things, via the horoscope pages and panoply of self-help and self-development books she had collected over the years, Bunty instantly assumed, waking up in a clammy sweat, that she was manifesting the guilt she felt about going behind Graham's back. What must Graham's dreams be like, she wondered. Waco massacres?

When she looked up 'I've murdered someone' in her dream dictionary, however, she was amazed to discover that this was the most common dream of all:

In the past, you buried some part of yourself, never allowing the real you to surface again. Now your subconscious is prompting you to free that element of your spirit that you have been denying yourself. It's time to be *you* again.

'But I don't know who me is,' she said to the curlicued page, before slamming the book shut and shoving it back into the bookcase, as if Graham might find it and somehow read her mind. Pearl and Finn of *On the Sofa* were chatting away in the background, and, not for the first time, Bunty found herself sitting across the studio from them, knees elegantly crossed on the slick leather couch, pushing her hair winsomely behind her ears as Pearl beamed at her.

Pearl: So, who *is* the real Bunty?

Bunty (*smiling*): That's a very good question, Pearl. I've been asking myself that a lot recently.

Pearl: And why's that?

Bunty: Well, my husband had the snip without telling me, and it set off this whole chain of events that had me wondering: Why am I married to this man? What do we have in common? And when it comes down to it, what do I have in common with anyone apart from other housewives these days?

Finn: He had the snip without telling you?

Pearl: Finn, trust you to focus on that. Bunty's baring her soul here. (*Turns to Bunty*). This issue of wondering where our real selves have gone is one that affects a lot of us as we approach middle age, isn't it? What did you used to enjoy that you aren't involved with any more?

Bunty: Well, ahem, sex.

Pearl rolls eyes understandingly and Finn starts to giggle.

Bunty: Nothing unusual. Going out. Live music. Having fun. Talking to other adults during the day about things other than children or the shopping list.

Pearl: And …

Bunty: Fencing! I love fencing.

Pearl: Well! That's unusual. And is fencing something you could pick up again?

26

Bunty: I need to. Right now. The guy's here to look at the drains.

Pearl: Pardon?

Finn rolls onto his side in abject mirth and Pearl, too, starts to giggle.

Bunty shook herself out of her reverie. She'd completely forgotten that the investigation of the constant pool of water at the bottom of the garden was due today. The excess moisture had churned up the mud near the fence to the extent that her lovely six-foot Waney Lap panels had toppled over in a light summer zephyr. There was no way it was going to survive the autumn, and while she could stomach an impromptu pond, she couldn't abide the thought of having to replace the wood she had so carefully creosoted then painted a denim blue. Graham was talking about concrete, for God's sake. She raced to the door.

'Sorry, just … on the loo,' she told the bemused drainage specialist.

'Fine. I'm Dan,' he said, holding out a hand, apparently without thinking twice about Bunty just having got off the toilet. He was probably up to his shoulders in crap every day anyway.

'Dan? Dan, Dan the drainage man.' Bunty clapped a finger to her mouth in an attempt to shut herself up.

He raised an eyebrow – an attractive auburn eyebrow, exactly the shade the cashier in the supermarket had been aiming for. 'That's me. Perhaps I could … have a look at the problem?'

'Yes. Yes!' Bunty pulled herself together and led him through the house and out into the garden.

Like so many gardens in the area, this was a small, fully enclosed space, half-decking, half-lawn, flanked by the odd rhododendron bush and some random bedding plants. Just to the side of one of the sorry-looking flowerbeds was the offending pool, Bunty's beautiful pine fencing panels leaning drunkenly towards it like Narcissus hoping to spot his reflection.

'I only noticed it when my fence got wobbly,' said Bunty, trying to recover from their introduction and sound at least a little sensible. The thought danced across her mind that Dan was probably very used to middle-class, middle-aged housewives simpering, losing their cool. He was rather attractive for a drainage man. Well, for any kind of man really.

Flexing his green uniform across his burly shoulders, Dan crouched down to study it more closely, looking left and right, and then poking a stick into the depth of it. Bunty tried to ignore his bottom, sitting atop the heels of his muddy boots like a pair of very edible cabbages. 'It goes down quite a long way. Suspect it's the overflow from the house behind, running up the road there.'

'Oh, that would make sense. It's Mary's garden. She hasn't been able to look after it properly since her husband died. It is fixable?'

He grinned. 'Everything's fixable, for a price.'

'Price doesn't matter, but can you save my fence?' Bunty looked down at him anxiously. 'I'm very fond of fences. I took a long time over this one.'

'It's … very nice.' Dan stepped around the puddle and studied the foundations. 'You might need new concrete posts.

These are quite crumbly.' Then he smiled at her. 'But I think your fence will be okay.'

Bunty smiled back. It was ridiculous, she knew, to be so concerned about a few panels of wood, but her very first job, her Saturday job, had been selling fencing in the local DIY store, and she had held an affinity for it ever since. The feeling of power brought about by being able to inform some rough-skinned, paunchy, middle-aged man (Graham, in fact) exactly what he needed to enclose his garden was completely enervating. She, a tiny fifteen-year-old, had known every variation of fixing, panels, trellises, and capping known to mankind. Womankind. It was hard to believe now, looking back. And for the first time she realised why she was so fond of her fences. For one, they made her feel safe. Contained, but prettily. But for another, they reminded her of the woman she used to be. 'The real me, Pearl,' she whispered.

'Sorry?'

'Nothing!'

'Oh.' Dan straightened from his prodding and squelching activities. 'I'll just get my camera.'

For a moment, Bunty thought he was going to take a picture of her. Why else would he want a camera? He was attracted to her! Wanted a memento. He might … might even kiss her. She could have sex! Well, why not, she thought, eyeing him surreptitiously. He really was quite tasty, and Graham was tarting around like a seventeen-year-old. What was to stop her? Apart from the fact that attractive drainage men probably got propositioned on a daily basis. She might catch something vile.

Just think where those hands were most of the day. And how very clichéd, how very Lady Chatterley.

It was only when he hauled up the iron square over the drain that she realised what he meant. 'Your special drainage camera.' Oh my God, she thought, groaning inwardly. What on earth was wrong with her head these days?

'Are you okay?' Dan stopped on his way to the van. 'You've gone a funny colour.'

'Just a … a hot flush.'

He almost winced visibly, and Bunty could have kicked herself again. Now she was menopausal in her late thirties? Nice. She leaned on the fence, fanning herself, as Dan's green back retreated up the garden. No doubt planning to leap into his van, drive away, far away, and never come back.

A light touch on her hand made her jump. 'Hello, Bunty. Are you all right?'

Mary's kindly wrinkled face was peering up at her from the garden behind. 'I was hanging out the washing and saw you there.'

'Mary, how are you?' Bunty still found it hard to talk to her lovely neighbour without a lump forming in her throat. It was ten or more months since Colin, her equally kindly husband, had fallen down in the supermarket with a stroke from which he had never recovered. Mary was still doing her washing every Tuesday, hanging out her sad, gigantic knickers that must have hung like flags without any wind on her rather wasted frame – another result of Colin's stroke.

Mary waved a pair at her. 'I'm fine thanks, love. Just hanging out my smalls. Is that man sorting your fence out?'

'Oh, Mary.' Bunty scratched her head. Where to start? 'He's a drainage man. We've got this pool of water in here, and he thinks it might be coming from your pipes.'

At that, Mary paled, her hand fluttering to her throat. 'Oh, love,' she said in tones of huge dismay. 'Will he have to dig up my garden? Only Colin spent so long on the borders, and Flinders is buried under the tree. And … oh, it'll cost a fortune, won't it?'

'It won't cost you a thing,' said Bunty firmly. This was some more tube cutting and diverting that Graham could bloody well pay for, as well as the exhumation and re-burial of Flinders, their tabby. 'And whatever happens, we'll make sure they respect everything. Everything.'

Mary nodded, mollified, her eyes slightly less rheumy than they had been a moment ago. 'Colin always dealt with all that stuff, you know. I'm good with the washing and the polishing and Victoria sponge, but tradesmen were always his area.'

'I know,' said Bunty gently. Theirs had been a happy division of labour, not like hers and Graham's.

Of course, at first she'd been content just to be looked after, post Adam. And then there'd been Charlotte. Then kitchen and bathroom renovations, fixing up the drive, painting fences. What exactly had she done for the last few years, though? Charlotte was at secondary school, barely there. Graham was at work, or squash (which she now took to mean 'at another woman's' or possibly 'in surgery'), and was also barely there. The house was

31

perfect, and so brimful of labour-saving devices that the housework practically did itself. What did she do? What was it that she, Bunty McKenna, actually contributed to this life? Whatever it was, or wasn't, it had created a pool of festering resentment, not unlike the stagnating puddle at her feet. But *Judge Judy*, *Trisha* and any number of daytime chat shows led her to believe that being there for the children was a worthwhile activity, that she should be recompensed enormously for the massive workload of sitting on her sofa watching … *Judge Judy*, *Trisha*, and any number of daytime chat shows.

'Better get on,' said Mary, tweaking on her clothes pegs. Bunty did so much of her drying in the tumble dryer that she would have been hard pressed to say where her paltry stock of clothes pegs actually was.

Suddenly Bunty grabbed the other end of the peg. 'Why? Why do you have to get on, Mary?' She probably looked rather feverish, and Mary did recoil slightly, but Bunty persevered. This was a time for change. For new routines. For not 'getting on', but actually getting off if the mood required it. 'Leave the washing. Go and get some of that Victoria sponge, and come and have a cup of tea with me.'

Mary looked confused, hesitant, and Bunty realised how much her routine meant to her. She clung to it as if she was hanging onto a bit of Colin. 'It'll start to smell if I don't hang it out. I'll just end up washing it again.'

'I've got a tumble dryer,' said Bunty. 'While we're having a natter, it will dry to a fluffy softness you could never imagine.'

Mary's eyes brightened. 'I've only got a bit of Bakewell tart.'

'Fantastic,' said Bunty. 'I'll put the kettle on.'

It wasn't much of a change, inviting a woman in her seventies round for English Breakfast (the closest Bunty had to 'ordinary' tea) and a slice of Bakewell tart – tart that the guest had to provide herself due to the sickening healthiness of Bunty's cupboards. But it was a start. It was something new. She was reclaiming her life. Her Buntyness. And it didn't involve shagging the gardener, which had to be a good thing.

But after her naughty hour with Mary, which they both enjoyed with the cheeky glee of kids playing hooky, she answered the phone to a slightly bigger change. A date, tomorrow, with a Croesus Club member called Jason.

She'd never heard of a rich man called Jason who wasn't a film star. And she couldn't even think, when it came to it, of too many of them, apart from the monster that leapt out of the lake in the *Friday the 13th* movies … Bunty shook her head. Too many movies. Too much TV. Too much goddamn imagination. It had always been a problem.

To: buntymckenna@ntsworld.com
From: admin@croesusclub.com
Dear Bunty,
Just to confirm the rendezvous with Jason, member 242, at The Pig and Cauli, tomorrow at 7.30 p.m.

As our consultant, Gemma, will have informed you, as responsible dating management practitioners, we would always advise that you tell someone where you are meeting and check with them afterwards that you are home safe and sound. Meet in an open, well-lit environment and do not invite your prospect to your home until you have had time to ascertain his character. Our vetting procedures, while very thorough, can only go so far.

Have a lovely time!
Priscilla.

To: admin@croesusclub.com
From: buntymckenna@ntswold.com
His surname isn't Dahmer, is it? Or Bundy?
Bunty

To: buntymckenna@ntsworld.com
From: admin@croesusclub.com
Hello Bunty
I'm afraid that according to our membership privacy protocols, I am not at liberty to divulge Jason's surname. If he wishes to tell you himself tomorrow, that is our member's prerogative.

Best wishes
Priscilla

To: admin@croesusclub.com
From: buntymckenna@ntswold.com
Sorry, Priscilla, that was another joke. B.

To: buntymckenna@ntsworld.com
From: admin@croesusclub.com
Dear Bunty
Your safety is never a joke to us.
Yours
Priscilla

To: admin@croesusclub.com
From: buntymckenna@ntswold.com
Hi P, no, I see that, of course, sorry. Sorry. B.

CHAPTER FOUR

Getting ready for a very furtive date was distinctly nerve-racking. Bunty was quite amazed that Graham actually had the stomach for it, but there he was, lumbering around in the corner of the bedroom, throwing white shorts and a rather armpitty polo shirt into a sports bag in readiness for his 'squash' game. Bunty wondered what, or who, he would be squashing, as she turned her nose away from the smell. He had this subterfuge down to a fine art, even packing shirts that had been pre-sweated in his attempts to con her.

'Right, that's me,' he said, zipping up the bag with a flourish. 'I think you could cancel Kristiana, you know. Charlotte can look after herself for an hour and a half until I'm home.'

Bunty covered her smile by swiftly applying some M•A•C Soft and Slow to her full lower lip. That made sense. If Kristiana were here with Charlotte, she couldn't be *there* with Graham. Or even here with Graham, with Charlotte apt at any moment to burst into the room demanding more food, more money, or more electricity for one of her vast array of technological devices.

'It's illegal,' she said eventually, as Graham stood with his hand on his hip – his more streamlined hip – waiting for an answer. 'She has to be fourteen before we can leave her on her own. And quite frankly she needs watching, unless …' She eyeballed Graham in the mirror. 'How do you spell vagina?'

There was a long pause. 'What?'

'Vagina.' Bunty said it in as slurred a fashion as she could manage without sounding like she'd been hitting the gin. Didn't want to give it away. 'How do you spell it?'

'More like: *Why* would I spell it?'

Bunty sighed. 'Just humour me, Graham.'

'All right,' he said with a slightly lascivious grin, looking up into the mirror like a kid at a spelling bee. 'Vagina: V … A … G …'

'Okay, it's not you.'

'It's not me?'

'No. Thank God.'

Big wiggling bums might still be Graham, but she was pretty sure he would know exactly how to spell that so the test was pointless. Shoving her eyeliner back in her makeup bag, she shooed him out of the room, ignoring his bewildered expression.

Downstairs, the pneumatic Kristiana had already commandeered the remote control and was fighting with Charlotte over whether to watch *The Simpsons* or *Project Runway*. Charlotte clearly favoured the latter. 'That gay guy totally loses it tonight,' she whined. 'I've been waiting all week to see it.'

'You are too young for gay guys and plunging necklaces,' purred Kristiana in her peculiarly American-tinged English.

'Necklaces? I'm too young for necklaces?'

'I think Kristiana meant necklines, Charlotte,' said Bunty from the doorway. 'And I agree. You are too young for gay guys and plunging necklines. And for looking up rude words on the computer.'

The brilliant flush that swept across Charlotte's pimples was all the evidence she needed, but Bunty was temporarily distracted by the appearance of Graham beside her. Would he give himself away?

'Don't worry, Charlotte,' he said. 'Your mum's losing it. She's just been asking me to spell rude words too.'

Kristiana raised a beautifully arched, golden eyebrow. The two together could have been used as an advert for Macdonalds. 'Mrs McKenna, I have a very good dictionary if you need to borrow it.'

'Thank you, but I know how to spell all the rude words I need to, thank you.' This wasn't going quite as planned. Instead of chastising her daughter and making sure the childminder wasn't bonking her husband, she was coming across as some kind of perverted schoolteacher. 'Look, never mind, just make sure Charlotte goes to bed before ten, doesn't go on the computer unsupervised, and doesn't watch anything she shouldn't, including Project Runway.'

'Aw, Mu-um …'

'I'll be back before ten anyway,' interjected Graham.

Bet you will, thought Bunty darkly. Quick grope in the downstairs cloakroom as he got Kristiana's coat for her – she could see it already. She just hoped Jason was going to be up to the challenge.

'What time are you back, darling?' said Graham solicitously.

'When I feel like it,' replied Bunty.

A slight frown passed across Graham's face, but once again Bunty ignored it as she blew a kiss towards Charlotte, who rolled her eyes, and headed out of the door. She clambered into her Mini Cooper, then paused. Here was an ideal opportunity to see what Graham was actually getting up to when he purported to play squash. Checking her watch, she found she had a full thirty minutes before her meeting with her mysterious millionaire, so she pulled down a side road and waited for Graham to ease by in the company Mondeo.

As soon as he'd gone by, Bunty pulled out again, sliding down in her seat, almost wishing for a headscarf and dark glasses. She rang Kat. 'Guess where I am?'

'At the pub? You've seen him already and can't decide whether he's the pig or the cauli.'

'No, I'm following Graham!'

'You don't have to whisper, Bunty, unless you're following him in the back seat of the Mondeo.'

They veered left towards the sports hall. 'Sorry. Oh, he's pulling in.'

'Where?' squeaked Kat.

'At the sports hall.'

Long pause. 'The sports hall where the squash courts are?'

Bunty peered around her bleakly. It was, in fact, the very same sports hall with squash facilities that Kat had just mentioned. Graham actually was playing squash. 'I don't believe it,' she said, watching Graham gather his battered squash bag from the boot. 'He can't be just playing squash.'

'Why not?' said Kat, not unreasonably.

'He just can't … Oh! Wait. He's not going in. He's waiting in the doorway. He's meeting someone. Kat! It's a woman! A bloody blonde woman and he's getting in her car. Shit!'

'Take a photooooo,' screeched Kat.

But Bunty was in too much shock to remember that she had a camera on her phone, let alone how to use it. He actually *was* having an affair. Her wild imaginings were right on the button. The tart even looked like Bunty had imagined, although the bottom was more firm and twangy than big and wiggling.

'Bunty?'

'Bastard!' Bunty threw the car into gear.

Kat's voice sounded extremely hopeful. 'Are you going to follow them?'

'No bloody way. He thinks I'm just going to take it while he pokes some blonde bint, does he?'

'So what are you doing?'

Bunty grinned viciously. 'Operation Shug D. I'm going to meet this Jason. And he won't know what's hit him.'

Kat giggled. 'Call me after. Or during if he's really creepy and you need an escape call.'

'Over and out,' snapped Bunty.

She fumed all the way to the Pig and Cauli, for the first time feeling hurt and trying to tot up all the times Graham had said recently that he was off to play squash. He'd even started going on Sunday mornings. That should have told her! Sunday mornings were sacrosanct to Graham – lying in bed too late, optimistically nudging Bunty's thigh with his half-erect penis, giving up and eating too much bacon on buttered toast. Such had

40

been their routine for years, ever since Charlotte had turned into the hormonally driven wreck that she now was and needed to sleep till midday.

'Squash. Ha!' muttered Bunty, walloping the car over one of the tree-filled concrete diamonds in the car park and berthing it diagonally in a disabled space. It was the only remaining parking spot under a light – that's what she'd say if anyone complained. Get Priscilla onto them maybe.

As she got out, she checked the other cars in the vicinity, hoping for at least a Silver Ghost, but finding only the usual selection of sales rep cars and more ladylike, hot hatches, including a rather flash-looking Golf in electric blue with a personalised number plate: JAMMY 23. She entered the pub, nerves masked by the outrage still pulsing through her courtesy of Graham's blatant betrayal.

There was no sign of Jason, just the usual collection of besuited twenty-somethings, notching up enormous tabs on their expense accounts. Bunty looked around. To her surprise, one of the twenty-somethings, stationed on his own in the corner of the pub, raised a hand.

'Hi. Bunty. You look just like your photo,' said the boy, wiping champagne out of the bum-fluff on his chin.

'You don't ... are you Jason?' Now that she looked again, there was a resemblance to the photo she had seen on the Croesus Club email, except that this version was only half the age of the person she'd imagined she'd be meeting.

'Yeah!' He laughed delightedly. 'Photo was of me dad. Thought it might go down better, you know.'

Bunty sat down with a bump. 'So you're not a city trader, dynamic, earning lots, looking for … well, me?'

Jason shrugged lightly, the thin wool of his suit creasing over his shoulders like vulture's wings. 'Oh yeah. I am. I'm all of those things. Super rich and all that. Jammy bastard, the other traders call me.'

He poured Bunty a glass of champagne – Moet, she noticed, doubtless the very best the Pig and Cauli had to offer – while the details sank in. 'Jammy. That's your Golf outside?'

'Jammy 23. My name, my age.'

'Oh, Jesus.' Bunty upended the glass, trying hard not to burp as the bubbles rushed down her gullet. 'You're twenty-three? That's …' That's what, she thought. Not much older than my daughter? Younger than my babysitter? Downright ridiculous?

'But … but you saw how old I am and everything,' she stammered at length.

'Oh yeah,' said Jason, folding his arms across his chest and leaning back in his seat. He looked like he was appraising a racehorse.

'So … why?'

Jason laughed, flashing an impressive set of expensive veneers. They were the most attractive thing about him. 'It's your age. Well, and you look good too. I like women your age. You're the capital of China, incha?'

Bunty shook her head. 'I'm … Beijing?'

At this, Jason tutted. 'Well, they would go and change it, wouldn't they? No, you're the old name for the capital of China.'

'Peking?'

Bunty was totally lost, but even more so when Jason leered distinctly at her crotch. 'That's right. Thirty-five. Peking, mate.'

Peking. She was Peking. Peeking? Or … 'Ohhhhh,' she said after a short period of tugging at her skirt to deflect Jason's lecherous glance. 'Peaking. I'm thirty-five, so I'm peaking.'

'Sexually,' said Jason with a nod and the faintest hint of a dribble.

She'd heard the myth, of course. Women reached their sexual peak at thirty-five, men at …. nineteen, was it? It didn't seem likely, somehow, bearing in mind the slightly spongy nature of her breasts and stomach. Her sexual prime had to have been before her boobs turned from Pippin's apples to small bananas. Surely someone younger, Kristiana for instance, was 'peaking'. Bunty was over the summit and down the other side. In fact she was fairly sure she'd read somewhere that Watchit and Perv, or whoever had done the survey in the fifties, had come to this conclusion because the only women they could get to talk about sex, even admit to knowing anything about it, where in their mid thirties. Now people struck up casual conversations about it on the bus, opened up their blogs for all to see, even broadcast documentary accounts of their lurid and tasteless foragings on *YouTube*. Netnurse. Must get Netnurse, she reminded herself. Even that sounded vaguely tainted.

'I lied,' she said eventually. 'About my age. I'm thirty-eight. Peaked. Completely peaked. Over the bloody hill and in a pit at the bottom.'

Jason didn't look perturbed. Nor did he look like someone who could get a shag by normal means. 'You still look pretty lusty to me.'

Bunty covered her mouth in an attempt not to giggle. Bloody Priscilla was going to die. 'But Jason, or can I call you Jammy? Jammy, you must have known from my profile that I'm actually looking for a husband, not just a … a fling.'

To her great consternation, Jason leaned over the table and squeezed her fingers. 'Well, I was thinking we might do ourselves a little deal. I'm a trader, see. I know my markets.'

'Your markets?' Bunty slid her hand out from under the boy's sweaty fingers, hoping desperately that nobody she knew ever came into the Pig and Cauli. She fumbled furtively for the speed dial on her mobile. Come on, Kat.

'It's just like a business deal, isn't it?' Jason winked. 'I got the money, you got the looks and the … peaking, sexual, grrrrrr stuff. Thing is, I'm always going to have the money, and you're not always going to have the looks, so it's not much of a deal for me if I end up being your husband, is it? So I thought we might treat it like a sort of … leasehold venture.'

Bunty spluttered champagne right down her front. 'You want to … to rent me? There's a name for that, you know?'

'No, not like that.' Jason held up a hand. 'You're making it sound, you know, cheap. What I'm proposing is an old-fashioned, mutually beneficial business deal.'

Kat, call me back, call me back, thought Bunty desperately. So this was what she had to look forward to – youths barely out of puberty expecting ping-pong tricks from a desperate older woman. It might work for men, copulating with women half their age who still had firm high breasts, manuals on giving blow-jobs and vaginas like a length of hose pipe, but the prospect of clambering into bed with someone who still had regular wet dreams was too depressing by half. So depressing, in fact, that she wasn't going to stand for another second of it.

'Jason, let me tell you a bit about the business you're trying to get into.' Bunty planted her hands on the table. 'First of all, all the money in the world would not persuade me to sleep with you. In any kind of deal, as far as I'm aware, your business partner needs to want something out of it too. And by the way, men – boys – peak at nineteen, so you're already past your sell-by date.' Jason's mouth fell open as Bunty picked up the champagne and tipped it neatly into his crotch. 'Furthermore, if you're not very, very careful, you'll end up with warts on your willy, and nobody will want to do business with you, ever, ever again. Good night.'

And she stalked off across the pub, hardly aware of Jason's admiring stare and his cold-crotched groan: 'I like your style! Come back!'

To: admin@croesusclub.com
From: buntymckenna@ntsworld.com
Priscilla
I think you should be aware that 'Jason' is actually a little boy wearing his dad's suit, and a sex maniac to boot. If I hadn't found it quite so funny I'd be highly offended at what went on at my rendezvous. Please tell me they're not all like that!
Bunty (which Jason/Jammy obviously thought meant 'Bounty')

From: admin@croesusclub.com
To: buntymckenna@ntsworld.com
Dearest Bunty,
I am disappointed that your meeting was not to your liking. Jason was rather taken with you and was hoping to meet with you again. If he does not meet with your approval, however, we will move on to your second rendezvous.
Priscilla

To: admin@croesusclub.com
From: buntymckenna@ntsworld.com
But Priscilla, he's 23!

From: admin@croesusclub.com
To: buntymckenna@ntsworld.com
And you're 38, I believe. Age is not a barrier to love, in our view.

To: admin@croesusclub.com

From: buntymckenna@ntsworld.com

Okay, okay. So I cut a couple of years off my age. He cut off a couple of decades! And it's not all he needs to cut off. Could the next one be someone who doesn't live with his mum?

CHAPTER FIVE

Bunty lay in bed, one eye open, eyeing up Graham in as surreptitious a fashion as she could. One of his Shrek ears had a red weal across it where it had been folded against the pillow, and she had to resist the unbearable urge to get the scissors out of the bedside table and cut along the line. It looked like one of those paper cutouts that with a few deft folds would turn into a pyramid, or a swan. Maybe a small pig, given the porcine nature of the wobbly top of Graham's ear.

There was much less of him that wobbled though, she noticed. The mounds under the duvet were definitely lower in profile – the Pennines instead of the Cairngorms. Or more like those things they use to talk about in O-level geography – drumlins, was it? Little hills like a basket of eggs. Bunty's mind went off in two directions at once, one part visualising Graham's body as containers of various eggs, all shrouded by the duvet. His legs and feet were links of half Easter eggs, like the Flower Pot men; his body a washing basket like Mary's piled high with ostrich eggs; his head one enormous dinosaur egg, the ridiculous ears stuck on too low, too much at right angles.

Her other train of thought chugged through the mystery of adolescent exams. She doubted very much whether anyone Charlotte knew remembered O-levels, 'A-levels, and even S-levels for the uber-clever like Cally had been. In fact, she doubted whether any of Charlotte's teachers even remembered O-levels. It was all rather worrying, as she wasn't entirely – no, not even slightly – au fait with what had taken their place. GCSEs seemed to be some combination of the exams Bunty had done at school, but there was so little emphasis on them these days. Charlotte, she was sure, could get a high grade just from turning up most days and avoiding getting arrested at the mall, yet she clearly wasn't lacking in intelligence. She'd hacked into the computer like a pro, for Christ's sake. Netnurse. Remember the Netnurse.

'Why are you looking at me like that?' Graham had the matching eye open and was now watching her across the pillow. 'Fancy a bit?'

'Since you put it so nicely,' said Bunty, deepening the duvet valley between them, 'no thanks.'

'Bunny,' crooned Graham. 'Come on, it's been ages. And you've got that look in your cyc.'

How little he knew her, to somehow mistake parental concern for lust. 'You're sick,' she said, then stopped.

It wasn't entirely fair to assume that he'd known what she was thinking; sometimes she hardly knew herself what she was thinking these days. Too much time on her own had somehow turned her into Walter Mitty. What would the female of Walter be? Waltette? Walta? And there she went again, inventing a new persona for herself – borrowing an old persona and turning it into her own, in fact. Whatever the case, she was back inside her head, not in bed with her husband, whose increasing libido seemed to be snaking through the duvet valley and nibbling at her thigh.

'Graham, no,' she said softly.

He looked at her once, wounded, and turned onto his other side.

Serves you right, she thought viciously. Expecting me to come up with the goods when you're porking some Lycra-bottomed bimbo from the squash club. It was quite possible that it was last night's indiscretions that had given him this extra boost in the first place. She distinctly remembered Kat telling her in the throes of an affair with her married boss that she could take the claim for reviving their love life. Not hers and the boss's, but the boss and Mrs Boss's. 'I was so happy after shagging you and it all going so well that I actually went home and boffed my wife!' he'd told her in tones of great pride. Needless to say, the affair didn't last much longer, and Kat quickly said goodbye to the boss, her bonus and ultimately her job.

So maybe this was where Graham was at right now. Some blockage had been cleared. It had, after all, been some months since they'd got round to anything other than a cursory kiss on the cheek in the morning. He'd got his plunger out, cleared the drain, and he was off. Which reminded her. 'Oh my God, Dan will be here in five minutes.'

Graham sat bolt upright. 'Dan? Who the hell's Dan?'

And who the hell's Lycra-bum, Bunty wanted to retort, but instead she smiled mysteriously. 'Just a man I need to see. Isn't it time you were going?'

Graham's eyes narrowed, then he threw back the duvet in a huff. Bunty watched, bemused, as he made a huge show of putting on his shirt, stowing his arms in the sleeves bicep-up, slowly, one arm deliberately after the other, sucking in his gut so the outline of his ribs was the last thing to disappear under the white cotton as he buttoned his shirt from the bottom up.

She propped herself up on her elbow. 'Have you been at that lap dancing club again?'

'I've never been to one,' said Graham, throwing a sly glance in her direction. 'Why, was that sexy?'

At which Bunty howled with laughter as she clambered out of bed. It had actually reminded her of shoving a pillow into its case. 'Yes, darling. You red hot lover, you.' She patted his stomach – definitely smaller – and headed for the ensuite.

When the bell rang a few minutes later Charlotte beat her to the door. Bunty could almost hear her hormones surging from halfway up the stairs.

'Hi, I'm Dan.'

'Oh, hi-i-i-i-i. I'm Charlotte, but call me Charlie.'

Charlie? When had that come about? She'd been Lottie as a little girl, then Charlotte since seven or eight (and an introduction to *Charlotte's Web*). The heaving-bosomed teen version of her daughter was reinventing herself yet again. She had a genetic predisposition towards it, after all.

'Thank you, Charlotte,' said Bunty, throwing open the door to a slightly pink-faced Dan, studying his bucket rather hard in an attempt to avoid Charlotte's appraisal of his shoulders and lightly stubbled chin. 'Dan, why don't you go down the side path?'

'Sure.' Dan took off with alacrity down the gravel path at the side of the house, while Charlotte chewed on a piece of hair.

Bunty slapped her fingers out of her mouth. 'Shouldn't you be at the bus stop?'

'I'm too late. Can I have a lift?'

'No.' It was too bad, and a hard lesson to learn, but Charlotte was already far too willing to wait for everything to be handed to her on a plate, preferably in metallic fuchsia pink. Where she'd got that attitude from was hard to establish. 'You'll just have to be late. You'll get in trouble, maybe even get a detention, and then you'll know that next time you have to get yourself ready in time.'

'You're growing up now, Charlotte. We won't always be here to pick up the pieces, Charlotte. You have to start to do things for yourself, Charlotte,' whined her daughter, finishing Bunty's lecture for her with almost the exact words she had been about to use. 'Thing is, Mum, you don't like it when I do things for myself really, do you?'

'Don't talk rubbish. Go to school,' said Bunty abruptly.

'I'll take you, Char,' said Graham, wafting down the stairs in a breeze of some new aftershave. Some expensive new aftershave, unless she was very much mistaken. She'd only just trained him out of the overpowering astringency of Lynx, and now he was shopping at the Gucci store? She felt a grudging admiration for Lycra-bum.

'Graham, I'm trying to teach her a lesson.'

'I'm going past the door.' Graham straightened his tie in the mirror and waved Charlotte on. 'Teach her a lesson tomorrow.'

Charlotte shot Bunty a small, triumphant glance then plumped into the passenger seat.

'Both of you,' said Bunty under her breath. 'I'll teach both of you a lesson.'

They both deserved one, in her view, having both struck a nerve. That Graham – perfumed, provocative, posturing Graham – was due his comeuppance was a given. And Charlotte? Well, it was true that the last time Charlotte had taken matters into her own hands it had been on a rather spectacular scale. After overhearing one of their arguments when Graham had accused Bunty of 'getting off' with Cally's then boyfriend (now, oddly, Cally's stepson), Charlotte had taken it into her head that she was the love-child of the liaison that never was. She was fairly sure she would not be able to investigate herself, so she had inveigled her younger friend Paige – Alan's *actual* love child – into collecting DNA for her to do a paternity test. In New Zealand – *CSI: New Zealand*. For the millionth time in the last few days, it occurred to Bunty that Charlotte knew far too much about biology.

Dan's face swam into view. 'Could you hook me up?' Hook me up? Wasn't that what Charlotte's generation called getting together for a shag? Booty call, hooking up, friends with benefits – a whole range of unfathomable, uncommitted, sleazy options for the modern courtship. She should have taken lessons from Jason the Jammy.

Dan wanted to be hooked up with her? Bunty's breath caught in her throat. It was a very tempting thought. He was a bit younger than her, for sure, but not a decade and a half. He liked fencing. He had that rugged outdoors look – no stripy arms from tanning in a sleeved T-shirt, just the slightly ruddy look of someone who spent a lot of time outdoors. Or maybe it was rust. Or worse, thought Bunty, suddenly remembering that Dan was not a sensitive Diarmud Gavin gardener type, heaving concrete one day and delicately stroking a cyclamen petal the next. This was Dan. Dan, the drainage man, up to his armpits in crap most days.

'Um, kitchen tap?' Dan waved the hosepipe under her nose.

'Oh! Oh, yes, hook up the hose. I'll … I'll meet you at the back window. Near the sink. Kitchen tap. Right there.'

Dan nodded slowly. 'Right. Back window. Are you … are you okay?'

'Yes! Fine. Sorry, just a bit distracted.' By your curiously blue eyes and black eyelashes. No! 'Bit of an argument with my daughter.'

With something that looked very much like relief, Dan nodded vigorously. 'God, they're hard at that age, aren't they? My son's fourteen. Sometimes I wonder if we're even related. I think my ex had an affair with Ronnie Biggs. He's like this small criminal mastermind.'

'You have a fourteen-year-old son?'

'I know, I know. Don't look old enough, do I?' Dan leaned on the doorframe with a cheeky grin. 'I was only twenty when he was born.'

'First girlfriend?'

'Nah!' Dan laughed. 'First proper relationship, though. We lasted eight years. Not bad these days, is it?' He smiled again, disarmingly frank.

He was nice, Bunty decided. Their expectations of life were completely different. For her marriage had meant forever, and the house, and the two cars, not 'anything over five years is good enough'. But she liked him, nonetheless. Dan was honest, cared about his son, worked hard at his job ... And waited patiently for distracted women to attach his hosepipe to the water supply.

'Back window,' she said again, and closed the front door.

Mary was peeking meekly over the tumbledown fence when Bunty joined Dan for his verdict. 'Is it in my garden?' she asked, her voice quavering.

'Dan, this is Mary, my ... friend,' said Bunty. Dan wiped his hand, then reached across the fence and shook Mary's delicate veined fingers. 'Dan's just seeing exactly what happens when the water goes through. Is that right, Dan?'

He nodded. 'I had a poke around with the camera last time I was here, but it was a bit inconclusive. Thought I'd try it the old-fashioned way, with water. The only trouble is, I can't feed the hose through under the fence. The hole's too small.'

Bunty gave Dan's hands a furtive glance. They were enormous, twice the size of her own. One false shove with one of those and her fence would be over in a second. 'Allow me,' she said, and got to her knees.

The tiny grid covering the offending pipe was sitting in the tight angle between the ground and the leaning fence, which was now so far over that a rush of wind from Mary's rapidly rotating dryer could push it right to the ground. Grabbing the end of the hose from Dan, Bunty winkled her way under her prized, denim-blue Waney Lap, head first, on her elbows. She felt like an action hero – Angelina Jolie, or someone – belly-crawling into 'Nam,' planting the decoy, saving her side from sure decimation. With her cheek to the damp ground, she finally lay alongside the grid. As gently as if it were a hand grenade, she levered off the metal lid and nosed the hosepipe down into its depths.

She wriggled out, bottom first. 'Done,' she said, brushing herself down. 'I'll go and turn the tap on.'

Dan and Mary waited with matching admiring expressions as Bunty trotted up the boggy garden and into the kitchen. She watched for the thumbs up, leaning against the sink. Dan and Mary were in deep conversation, then Mary headed off into her own house and Dan made his way towards Bunty.

'It's definitely in Mary's garden,' said Dan through the open kitchen window. 'This little spring developed right beside the apple tree.'

'Her cat's buried there,' said Bunty, nodding. 'They must have disturbed something when they put Flinders in the ground.'

'Oh God.' Dan dropped his head onto his hands. 'That is the worst of this job. I can stand all the shit – 'scuse me – and the smell and everything, but having to tell little old ladies we need to dig up their kitty is just awful.'

Bunty smiled. What a gentle giant. A sweet, brightly shining, rough diamond. 'I'll tell her,' she said.

'She's gone to get cake,' said Dan with a groan.

'Well, then, you'd better wash your hands,' said Bunty, with a lift in her heart. Everything was not rosy in the garden, but suddenly life was beginning to look a whole lot brighter. There were options. 'I'll put the kettle on.'

To: admin@croesusclub.com
From: buntymckenna@ntsworld.com
Hi Priscilla,
You've been really really kind and everything, setting me up with Jason, but I think I'm going to pull out now. Thank you for all your help.
Kind regards
Bunty

From: admin@croesusclub.com
To: buntymckenna@ntsworld.com
Dear Bunty,
Oh, that's a shame. You know we give you three chances, and we have someone lined up who we think would be just perfect for you: 38, yachtie, tall dark handsome, Kiwi. Tra la la! Good luck with your endeavours.
Yours,
Priscilla
P.S. I hate to mention this, but I am bound to state that any further meetings with Jason will count as a successful match, and you will be charged the full Love-Lottery fee.

From: buntymckenna@ntsworld.com
To: admin@croesusclub.com
P, I cannot state this more strongly – I would rather glue my eyeballs round the wrong way than ever see Jason again. And

the kind of fees you should be charging for him are of an entirely different (and dubious) nature.

All the best though,
Bunty.

From: buntymckenna@ntsworld.com
To: admin@croesusclub.com
Hmmm. Actually, Priscilla, could I rethink this one? We like Kiwis. One of my friends has a child by one, and another by his father, and my other friend is going out with the first friend's ex. Good sign, huh?

Bunty

From: admin@croesusclub.com
To: buntymckenna@ntsworld.com
Dearest Bunty,
I don't really know how to respond to that. I am now tempted to tell you that the Kiwi is taken, but I am somewhat tied up in protocol.

Priscilla

From: buntymckenna@ntsworld.com
To: admin@croesusclub.com
Admittedly, P, it does sound a bit weird, but it is all very, very above board. How about I don't mention my date with the juvenile delinquent again, and you set me up with the Kiwi.

Does he have a name, by the way?
B

From: admin@croesusclub.com

To: buntymckenna@ntsworld.com

Agreed. Ben will be available this Friday evening at the Connoisseur Wine Bar, 7.30 p.m. I'm assuming that I do not need to repeat our safety recommendations.

Priscilla.

From: buntymckenna@ntsworld.com

To: admin@croesusclub.com

No, all dutifully remembered. Will be taking a small SWAT team to sit outside, ready to swoop.

B

From: buntymckenna@ntsworld.com

To: admin@croesusclub.com

That was a joke by the way. Again.

From: admin@croesusclub.com

To: buntymckenna@ntsworld.com

I realised that, Bunty, hence the lack of a reply. I am not without a sense of humour myself, you know. But I do have other clients to attend to. Good luck with Ben.

Priscilla.

CHAPTER SIX

The guy in the window seemed unfeasibly good-looking. Bunty pretended to reapply her lip gloss while she took another furtive glance into the Connoisseur. There didn't appear to be any other single men in the bar, from what she could glean through the artfully designed gloom, although there were several sets of single women edging their way closer to him. One actually dropped her menu near his feet, then beamed with orthodontic glamour at the lone male as he scooped it up and handed it back to her.

'Hands off, he's mine,' Bunty muttered, clambering at last out of the car.

Hands off, he's mine. Who had sung that? She almost started strutting to a ska-reggae beat as she approached the doorway. The Specials? It was definitely someone ska-ish. 'Until the end of time …' Not 'he's mine'; it was 'she's mine'. A male band. An eighties, ska-type, black-and-white … Through the door, past the salivating females, over to 'Tall, Dark and Handsome' in the corner. Reach out for his hand.

'The Beat!' she exclaimed, seizing his fingers.

'No,' said the man slowly, cocking his head. 'I'm Ben.'

Bunty's skin flared scarlet. 'Oh God, I'm sorry. I know. I'm Bunty. I was just thinking who sang that song, 'Hands …', um, this song, and I just remembered it was The Beat.'

'Hands off, she's mine,' said Ben with a grin. 'I loved that song. All that ska-reggae stuff.'

'It was just on the radio.' Bunty fanned her face as she took the seat he'd pulled out for her. No need to explain what had actually been going through her head. 'It's not how I normally greet people.'

Ben gave her a small grin. 'I like it. Different. The kind of greeting you don't forget in a hurry – straight into a pop quiz.'

He poured her a glass of the rather expensive Chablis he had chilling at the side of the table, and Bunty checked him out. He really was quite good-looking – a broad, tanned face, dark hair, eyes so dark brown they were practically black and a hard, rugby player's body. Of course, it was a bit of a cliché to imagine that all Kiwis played rugby preceded by poky-tongued war dances, like the All Blacks in the Rugby World Cup (which Graham had insisted on watching, although he'd not been near a rugby ball in aeons). But she could certainly imagine Ben's shoulders barging in among the others in a scrum, the thighs straining against the hem of his little white shorts, those impossibly dark eyes sparking competitively. Get a grip, Bun, she told herself sternly.

'Thank you.' She took the wine and raised her glass at Ben. 'So, um, go on then, what would your pop quiz question be?'

'Easy. I always ask Poms this, and they never know. What was the name of the famous New Zealand band headed up by the Finn brothers in the early eighties?' He raised an eyebrow.

'I know! I know! Crowded House. I loved Crowded House.'

Ben pretended to wrestle the wine glass from her hand. 'No, no, no. That was the nineties. Split Enz.'

'Oh! Of course. Split Enz.'

How could she forget? 'I got you' was one of the many covers that Adam and his band had done. Badly, of course. Adam himself had some talent as a singer and writer, accompanied by some mediocre guitar playing, but in a place the size of Taunton it had been fairly difficult to garner enough talent to make up a band that was ever going to really take off.

But here was Ben, grinning at her rather winsomely and looking distinctly as though he was enjoying the prospect of spending an evening with her. And hadn't Priscilla mentioned a boat? 'So you're a yachtie.'

'Brought up in Auckland, the City of Sails, it's hard to be anything else,' said Ben. 'I've just spent the last six months sailing round the world, ending up here. I hope this place was all right for you to meet up?'

Here. On the yacht. Drinking champagne. Trailing hands in the water, brushing each other's fingers. It all sounded completely splendid. 'It's fine here,' said Bunty with a smile.

'And you have quite an unusual hobby yourself. Fencing? I'll have to get you cutting and thrusting on the yacht.' Ben waved for a waiter with menus. 'Very Keira Knightley.'

Bunty groaned as she pictured the *Pirates of the Caribbean* scene he was envisaging. 'Oh, no, it's not that …' Wait a minute, though. Ben was evidently rather intrigued by the comparison. It might have been the one reason he was interested in her – some elaborate male fantasy involving rapiers, flowing white shirts, and masked women. What the hell. 'Yes, it's just a little something I got interested in when I was younger.'

'Pop quizzes and fencing.' It came out as 'fincing', in much the same way that his name had sounded like 'Bin'. 'You're quite an unusual woman, Bunty.'

She let out a slightly hysterical laugh. 'You have no idea, Bin. Ben. No idea at all.'

In response, he clinked his glass against hers and drained it in one gulp. 'Let's eat,' he said, in a tone that was masterful, enquiring, solicitous and hungry all at the same time.

Over dinner, Bunty discovered that the trip around the world had been an escape from a messy break-up. Ben's wife, inexplicably in Bunty's view, had been having an affair, a totally clichéd affair with his work associate. (Co-owner of the yacht? She'd find out later.) It was hard to imagine how his wife could have found someone preferable to Ben to shack up with. 'My husband's having an affair, too,' she said, just touching the end of her finger against his.

'Having?'

Shit. 'Well, had, obviously, not still having, because we're not together any more. So quite honestly I don't know what it's called now. It was an affair; now I suppose it's a … a what? A relationship?' That was what it would be when it came to the crunch. A relationship. Happy Christmas from Graham and Lycra-bottom. Drinks and canapés at Graham and Lycra-bottom's. Wedding invitation: Graham, Lycra-bottom.

Ben put his head on one side, sympathy in his eyes for her babbling and incoherent state. 'He's really hurt you, hasn't he?'

'Yes,' replied Bunty automatically. Had he, really? She wasn't entirely sure. He'd denied her the chance of having any more children, that was true. Although it was also true that she had clearly stated she didn't want any more like Charlotte. And there was a certain proprietorial indignation, coupled with the sensation of mystery that someone else could actually find Graham attractive enough to want to take him away from her. When had *she* stopped finding him that attractive? Or, when it came down to it, when had she started?

'Do you have kids?' he asked.

Even though she was fairly sure this had been part of the profile, Bunty paused for a moment before replying. According to what she'd noted in his profile, he had two children, young. And he'd taken off across the world to chase out the ghosts of marriages past. It was another pop quiz question, the answer to which could either make him a) melt completely into a limpid puddle, b) practice a little more caution or c) run back to the yacht, hoist his mainsail and zip right back to New Zealand at a rate of many knots.

No answer, however, was not an option. 'One,' she said. 'Charlotte. She's thirteen. She's *really* thirteen.'

Darling Charlotte. A complex child from the outset, she had become even more charismatic of late. Conspiring with her friend to get someone's DNA was only one of the strange things she'd done recently, but Bunty supposed that slamming doors, hibernating for days with her iPod and a pizza box, and drawing strange black pictures of her parents swinging from the rafters were all just part of the usual bag of tricks that came with being a teenager.

Ben laughed. 'Poor you. Mine are five and two. Much easier to look after, I suppose.'

'At least I don't have nappies to deal with.'

'True.'

There was an awkward silence, during which Ben gazed through the etched glass onto the pavement outside. 'You must miss them,' said Bunty. It had to be six months since he'd seen them, unless … God, unless he'd kidnapped them and stashed them away on the boat, *yacht*, and was currently being sought in several different countries, extradited, entries on Match.com looking like a genuine convict .

'Yeah,' he said simply. There was just a glint of a tear in the onyx pools of his eyes. 'And Charlotte? Does she live with you?'

The question took her completely by surprise, though why it should she had no idea. It was a very natural question in this situation, in this day and age. If … when … Graham left her, it would be the most important discussion they would have. Where would Charlotte live? Who would have custody? Joint custody, sole custody, shared custody – these were all phrases that Bunty could not quite believe she was going to have to get involved with. And there was no obvious answer. Charlotte needed them both – her mum and her dad. Graham didn't cope too well with the parenting thing when left to his own devices, as evinced during their brief separation the year before. And yet Charlotte didn't live easily with Bunty either. Maybe they were too alike. Perhaps they fought for Graham's attention. Their gorgeous, much-loved daughter needed them both and somehow wanted neither. This was what Graham's betrayal had led them to.

'Bastard,' she said hoarsely, only then becoming aware that Ben was looking at her, frowning, waiting for but not wanting to push her into an answer.

'Are you sure … is this a good idea?' Ben touched her hand gently. 'Are you ready to get into something new?'

Hmm, let me think about this, she wanted to say. Gorgeous man? Check. Right age? Check. Rich? Cheque. Hurt and slightly vulnerable guy needing someone to pick him up, to fall in love with, who could completely empathise with the whole thing of being cuckolded? Double, triple, quadruple checkity check. 'Well,' she said eventually, 'it might be a bit soon. But I'm willing to risk it. If you are.'

He rewarded her with such a grin that her heart nearly fell into her napkin.

To: admin@croesusclub.com
From: buntymckenna@ntsworld.com
Dear Priscilla.
I think I love you.
Bunty

To: buntymckenna@ntsworld.com
From: admin@croesusclub.com
Dear Bunty,
I am truly hoping this time that this is one of your jokes as I am not of that persuasion, and it is not something you listed on your profile. We have been known to make matches of the same-gender variety, but there are agencies better suited to your proclivities if that is what you're seeking. I could recommend a few?
Priscilla

To: admin@croesusclub.com
From: buntymckenna@ntsworld.com
P, of course I'm joking, you daft tart. Don't you know me by now? Maybe what I should have said is that I love him – Ben. Well, not love, yet, but boy, a mighty good start. Bx (that's just a polite letter kiss, BTW, not a proper lezzy type kiss) for you.

To: buntymckenna@ntsworld.com
From: admin@croesusclub.com
I see. I am glad your meeting went well. I will charge the Love Lottery fee to your Visa card account.
Priscilla.

To: admin@croesusclub.com
From: Bunty McKenna@ntsworld.com
Hold your horses, Priscilla! We've not even had a second date yet! I'll let you know when we announce the engagement and perhaps you can charge us both then?
Bunty

CHAPTER SEVEN

Kat insisted on a complete low-down over a bottle of the same Chablis that Ben and Bunty had drunk, only this time they sat at the kitchen counter, both looking out at the view of the garden. Conveniently, the vista included Dan's muscular arms feeding drainage pipes under the fence, once again aided by Bunty's initial insertion. Casting aside the images of buckets and high colonics from some programme on the Living Channel – *How to Live with Your Parasites* or some such – she'd felt instead like a nurse to his surgeon, taking the pipes from him, operating in the dank flower bed, which was now starting to rot down in the shade of the teetering fence. He'd thanked her effusively when she stood and brushed her hands on her jeans. 'Mission accomplished, cap'n.'

'You're fantastic,' he said, rubbing her shoulder. 'What a woman.'

Kat observed all this from the window as she opened the bottle – it was Saturday afternoon, after all. 'He has totally got the hots for you!' she hissed as Bunty came back into the kitchen. 'Working on a Saturday and everything, and completely checking out your butt.'

Bunty smiled a trifle immodestly. 'I'll wear my really short tennis shorts next time.'

'Well, you don't need them for tennis.' Kat swirled her glass at Bunty, who ignored the tennis barb and sloshed another few inches of Chablis out of the bottle. 'Anyway, tell me about all these men. These *other* men, I mean. What about Jammy Dodger?'

'Him. I wouldn't be surprised if he was in the same class as Charlotte.'

Kat arched an eyebrow. 'What did you say on your profile? Perhaps he had you down as one of those pumas.'

'Pumas?' Bunty ran through the archive of TV shows in her head and plumped for a Tyra Banks Special. 'I think you mean cougars. Older women with younger men. Euw!'

'Nothing wrong with younger men,' said Kat. 'Half the women at work are shagging a bloke half their age.'

'He must be very tired.'

'And both parties seem to like it,' continued Kat pointedly.

Bunty sighed loudly so that Kat had to refocus her gaze from Dan's flexing shoulders to her face. 'That's the thing though, isn't it – they're *shagging*. I don't want shagging. I want a relationship. I need … *need* a husband.'

Kat leaned over and patted her hand. 'Bun-bun, whether it's a puma boy or a husband, there is going to be shagging involved.'

Bunty sighed again. Did Kat have a one-track mind at the moment, or was she being deliberately obtuse? Either way, sex was not the point. It wasn't as if she didn't like sex, for crying out loud. She had been rather enthusiastic about it at one stage, even in the early days of Graham. Oddly enough, that had been an improvement on sex with Adam. The aspiring rock god had often been too out of it, too tired, or possibly – once Bunty had dared admit the truth to herself – just too sated to be bothered with anything other than a token fumble. Or maybe he'd just turned really house-proud and didn't fancy copulating in the crusty Bri-nylon sheets of the latest Devon B & B. Nah. That didn't seem likely. But it had definitely had an impact on Bunty's libido being able to lie in bed in a post-copulation glow knowing that the sheets were clean on, were good quality British Home Stores, and would not be visited by any woman other than herself in the near future.

And let's face it, she mused, Graham had tried pretty hard. What he lacked in imagination he made up for in perseverance and willingness to please his new, exotic girlfriend. Bunty sometimes swore that her feet had been a size bigger prior to the nightly foot rubs that Graham had insisted on applying himself to, complete with exfoliant and Chanel No 5 body lotion, after a casual comment that reflexology could improve a woman's orgasm. Of course, of late she'd have been happy to settle for just the foot rub. If Graham didn't touch her anywhere above the ankle then that would have suited her just fine. It had all become a bit staid. A bit samey. A bit … well, a bit Grahamy. But with someone new, some new buffed paramour, Bunty reckoned it would be quite easy to regain that former vigour.

So no, it wasn't the shagging that was the point. It was the *not* shagging. Any old trout could get someone into bed. It took a different set of skills altogether to bag a rich husband, and even though the thought of leaping into a hammock with Ben was very tantalising, she had a vague feeling that the way to get a man in the Croesus Club would be to refuse to sleep with him.

Not for ever, obviously. Just until the ink had dried on the marriage certificate.

Dan appeared at the window. 'Would a cat be buried in a small cardboard box?'

'Oooh oooh hooo,' bleated Kat, leaning across the sink and crushing her enormous breasts together so that her cleavage ran up to her chin. 'I certainly hope not!'

'Dan, this is Kat,' said Bunty, as Dan looked blankly from one to the other of them.

His face cleared. 'Oh, I see, you're Kat. Ha. No, I meant an actual cat. The camera's butting up against some soggy cardboard with a label on it.'

Bunty would have imagined that nothing short of pure teak with brass handles would have done for Flinders, but then she recalled that Graham had been in charge of Flinders' burial. 'Can you tell what the label says?'

Dan checked his hand-held monitor. 'Something like … Fiesta Fun, size … 3?'

'Condoms?' said Kat with a look of horror. 'They put Flinders in a condom box? How many must they have *used*? And size 3, I mean, that's probably quite big, isn't it? Imagine, little old Mary and that randy old Colin.'

'No, not condoms, Kat. Please!' Honestly, Kat clearly did have a one-track mind at the moment. Must be time for another trip to Auckland. Bunty pointed at her own tiny feet. 'Shoes. Summer shoes from the Clarks children's department. Graham must have given them the box.'

'Well,' said Dan with a wince, 'it's not holding together very well. And neither is the cat judging by the smell.'

'Oh God.' Mary would be devastated on all fronts. Flinders decomposing. The indignity of a cardboard box coffin. The blocked drains caused by bits of cat and cardboard. 'There's nothing for it,' she said eventually. 'Mary goes to her sister's on Saturday afternoons. We'll have to take Flinders out and never, ever tell her.'

At which point Kat suddenly remembered an urgent appointment and beat a retreat. So it was Bunty who found herself, half an hour later, in a tracksuit recycled from the coffee group running club, wellies recycled from the coffee group gardening club, and a pair of brand new Marigold rubber gloves, far from recycled as she mostly managed to avoid doing the cleaning herself. She wasn't sure why, on reflection; even with the prospect of coming across a dismembered moggie, it was really quite a lot of fun digging around in the dirt.

Dan leaned back on his spade. 'Right, that's it. If you just jump in the hole and lever it out, we should be able to get it out in one piece. Oh! Okay, two pieces.'

'It's only the lid,' said Bunty. Ankle deep in stinking water, she averted her eyes from the deeply disturbing image of Flinders minus his eyeballs and wedged the lid back on with a squelch. 'Quick, before Mary comes back,' she added.

Dan yanked her out of the hole with one tug of his enormous hand. 'You know, for a little person you're pretty … What's the word? Feisty.'

'Little person? Isn't that what you have to call midgets these days?' Bunty bridled, fairly sure she had seen something like that on *Boston Legal*. 'I am not a midget. Just short, that's all. With small feet.'

Dan grinned. 'That's what I said. Short. And feisty.'

For one awful minute she was reminded of Jammy Jason smirking at her across the champagne bucket. Was Dan possibly flirting with her? He was certainly looking her up and down in a fairly carnivorous way. 'Why are you staring at me like that?'

'You're sinking,' he said.

'Oh.' It was true. Flinders' grave was fast filling up with scummy brown water, and Bunty's heels were sliding into the sinkhole. She was now only up to Dan's waist again, and she averted her eyes politely from his crotch as he grabbed her under the armpits and pulled her clear of the mire with a loud and rather rude squelching sound.

It was in this tableau, Dan clutching Bunty under the arms, Bunty's feet barely touching the floor, and a rotting cat squashed in between them, that Mary found them as she approached silently on her Scholl orthopaedics. 'Oh, Bunty. Whatever are you doing?'

Bunty took in her appalled and wrinkly face. Goddamnit, she had to be the one who looked like the adulterer, didn't she? Why hadn't Mary caught Graham *inflagrante* in the flower bed? 'Mary, believe me this is not what it looks like.'

'It's not Flinders?' Mary's relief was palpable. 'Only I thought I recognised the shoe box.'

Dan let go abruptly. Clearly Bunty was on her own in this one. 'Ah. No. No, that is, in fact, Flinders. In the shoe box. You see, the hole ...' Bunty looked around desperately. 'The hole was filling up with water because of this blockage ... further down. I knew that Flinders was under there. And I know how he hated water.'

A small light appeared in Mary's opaque eyes as she fished in her handbag for a handkerchief. 'He did.'

Bunty stroked her arm. 'Remember that time he chased Charlotte's paper plane up in the tree and wouldn't come down because he was right over the pond?'

It had all been quiet sweet really. Charlotte was three, possibly four – certainly not school age at any rate – and it was a glorious early autumn afternoon, mellow as a peach. Graham had come home from work early to surprise them both, spurred on by the unexpected sunshine, and while Bunty sat at the kitchen table (it was before the renovations, the bar stools, the granite worktop) with the magazine he'd brought home and the cup of tea he'd offered to make, Graham had pushed Charlotte around the garden on her Teletubbies trike. When that descended into an argument, as Graham wanted to take the stabilisers off and Charlotte flatly refused to get on it again without its special La-La wheels, Bunty had stepped in, and the magazine was reinvented with her botched origami until, finally, one of the planes flew. And after it flew Flinders. When had Graham stopped doing things like that? Not arguing with Charlotte, which occurred on a fairly regular basis, but the little gestures. The magazines. The cups of tea. Did he just not do them any more, or did she not notice? Hard to know. All she did understand was that the little gestures were no longer enough. His gestures needed to be bigger, more pronounced. Anyway, she remembered, it would no doubt be Lycra-bottom getting his big gestures from now on. And his big everything else. Well, she was welcome.

Bunty's snort of contempt brought her back to the present. Mary, luckily, took it to be an emotional reaction to the Flinders story.

'He was up there for hours until Graham stood the ladder in the pond and got him down.' Mary smiled tremulously at Dan. 'Do you have cats?'

He shook his head, then said, 'But Bunty told me how much you loved Flinders, and how he would have hated to get wet, and she … she insisted on coming to get him herself. Said she'd help you find a nice spot for him somewhere else.'

Nice one, Dan, thought Bunty as she gave Mary a hug with her free arm. 'Let's dry him … I mean, leave him out here while we have a cup of tea and think of a new spot for him.'

'For Dan?'

Bunty passed Dan the box and herded Mary inside. 'Both of them.'

'You're a very nice drain man, young Daniel,' called Mary over her shoulder. 'I shall recommend you to all my friends at the bridge club.'

'I do general plumbing as well,' he shouted back hopefully.

'He is nice, isn't he?' said Mary to Bunty.

And Bunty smiled back at Dan as he brandished his spade and she flicked a hand surreptitiously towards the other side of the garden. 'He's very nice, Mary. A very nice drain man indeed.'

But then the phone trilled in her tracksuit pocket, and the deep rumbling of a Kiwi voice in her ear distracted her from drains and Dan and errant husbands in nanoseconds.

To: admin@croesusclub.com
From: buntymckenna@ntsworld.com
Priscilla, I am having a second date with Ben the Kiwi, and thought I should tell you, even though it's a weekend and I'm sure you're out doing something fabulous.
Cheers, Bunty

To: buntymckenna@ntsworld.com
From: admin@croesusclub.com
I am doing something fabulous, Bunty. I am doing my job. We have just instigated a three-date policy before charging the Love Lottery finders fee, so you'll be glad to hear that you won't have to pay it.
Yours, Priscilla

From: buntymckenna@ntsworld.com
To: admin@croesusclub.com
So … you don't think we'll get to a third date? That's a bit defeatist of you, if you don't mind me saying, Priscilla.
Bunty

To: buntymckenna@ntsworld.com
From: admin@croesusclub.com
Ah, silly me. I simply meant that you don't have to pay it yet. Enjoy your date!
Kind regards
Priscilla

CHAPTER EIGHT

Unfortunately the joyously anticipated date with Ben had to wait a day. Graham had *plans*.

'What plans?' Bunty wanted to wrestle the newspaper out of his hand and bat him across the head. How could he have plans? He never did anything on a Saturday night. And it would have to be this Saturday night, the one Saturday that Bunty wanted to get out. 'You never have plans.'

Charlotte snorted from her armchair, much to Bunty's surprise; she'd assumed her daughter was listening to her iPod. Instead, she was listening to them. 'Whaddya mean Dad never has plans. He's like the king of plans. The Prime Minister of Plan City. The Pope of Planning in Popedom …'

'Okay, I get it,' said Bunty.

'Good,' replied Charlotte, checking out her spots in the back of her iPod. 'Cos I couldn't think of anyone else who's, like, really important. Oh. What about the Arch Angel of Canterwotsit?' It was a clearly a rhetorical question, as she was already feeding her earphones back through her curtains of hair.

'Bishop. Archbishop of Canterbury.' Bunty frowned at her daughter. She'd managed to turn the head of the Anglican Church into a character from *Heroes*. What exactly did they teach them at school these days?

Anyway, she'd got distracted. Plans. That's what she'd been thinking about. Graham's plans. To be fair, Charlotte had a point. Graham did have plans – of the one-year, five-year and retirement variety. He pored over maps for hours prior to any journey or holiday, and took great delight in proving the *AA Route Planner* wrong, as if they'd ever listen or care. Plans for Christmas, Easter, Halloween, music lessons, any other extracurricular activities had all been beaten into strictly even shapes on the gigantic white-board of Graham's mind.

But that's all they ever were. Strategies for the future. Nothing about now. About spontaneity. About suddenly deciding without warning to go out on a Saturday night without his wife or his child. 'So where are you going tonight?' she asked after Graham had retreated back behind his newspaper.

The paper lowered, a quick flick that just allowed him to make pacifying eye contact before re-entering his shroud of lies. 'Actually, it's tomorrow as well. The team's playing away tomorrow – Coventry – so me and the lads are going up to give them a bit of support.'

It would all sound quite reasonable coming from someone else, but Bunty spotted the obvious flaw. 'What team? What 'lads'?'

'Um, Chelsea? They're in the semis for the cup final, you know.'

Clever, thought Bunty. Get me on the one thing you know I can't answer you back on. Sport – men's sport particularly – did not even enter her consciousness as entertainment. Tennis was necessary for her social standing; the gym was a means to an end – her rear end, to be exact, to stay in any kind of shape to be admired by drainage men and Kiwis. But sport as something requiring spectators? Pointless. Pointless and expensive, which was the one reason she was surprised Graham had introduced this into his routine.

'Right, so you're going to drive up and stay over in Coventry, at say two hundred pounds, and then pay forty quid for a ticket to go and see – What is it you usually call them? – 'eleven talentless pricks kick a sheep's bladder around?'' Bunty pulled the newspaper down. 'And what 'lads'?'

Graham sighed, but at least had the decency to look a little shifty. 'Ryan from the office has hired a mini-bus and we've all chipped in a bit. We're staying at his auntie's in Solihull, and Ryan's mate has a season ticket and he can't go so it won't cost me anything. And as for the talentless prick thing, well, I did think that, I'll admit. But then I started doing the financial planning for a league player and I changed my mind. Very savvy, half of these footballers. Look at Beckham.' He shook out his newspaper again. 'Happy now?'

No, she wasn't bloody happy, not happy at all. It had all come out a bit too easily. Well *planned*. An AA charted route through the land of lies. But even more than that, she couldn't now announce that she was going out. The date with Ben was off. It was only when she slipped into the kitchen to do some furtive texting via Priscilla that the irony of her behaviour hit her. Well, she decided, hitting the send button, she'd been driven to it. It wouldn't have crossed her mind to have an affair if Graham hadn't beaten her to it.

She watched him with narrowed eyes as he headed up the stairs to pack his bag, handing her the newspaper on the way. 'I didn't think you'd mind, Bunty,' he said, with a roundabout

81

attempt at an apology. 'It's your favourite telly night. You know I hate all that stuff. Thought you'd like to get me out of the way.'

'Oh, believe me I would,' said Bunty with rather more malice that she'd intended.

Graham looked slightly alarmed for a moment, as if she was actually foreseeing his demise, then stuck his meaty finger on the TV page. '*Search for a Superhero* at 7.30,' he said softly in a come-hither sort of a voice. '*You've Got Talent*, followed by *The New Pans People*, and two hours of Ant and Dec making stars wallow in gravy. What do you want me here for?'

Bunty allowed him a small smile. 'That's true. I would rather be here with Ant and Dec.' Or Ben, she thought wickedly.

Graham smiled back, relieved, and Bunty did a double take. Had his teeth changed? They looked straighter. And whiter. Or maybe they just appeared whiter against his more tanned skin. Tanned skin? She looked again and for a moment had a horrible mental image of Graham turning into Peter Stringfellow, but was distracted by him calling over the banister: 'Charlie, go and get that surprise for your mum.'

There was no reply, since Charlotte was obviously plugged into the mains, so Graham hollered one more time, while Bunty gave up and walked back into the lounge. Hands on hips, she stood in front of her daughter until Charlotte rolled her eyes and removed her earplugs. 'What?'

'Well, Charlie,' said Bunty with heavy irony. How come everyone knew about that apart from her? 'Your dad wanted you to get the surprise he had for me.'

'Oh. Here.' Charlotte fished down the side of the cushion and withdrew a squashed box of chocolates. 'These are for you while you're watching TV tonight.'

Bunty peered under the wrinkled Milk Tray lid. 'Half of them are missing.'

'I ate the ones you don't like.'

'How do you know which ones I don't like?'

'Du-uh. I'm your daughter, aren't I?' And with that indisputable truth, Charlotte tutted loudly, helped herself to the last coffee cream, and wandered out of the lounge.

For a long moment Bunty stood in the middle of her lounge-cum-dining room trying to decide which object to hang onto as the walls revolved around her. Who were these people, living in her house with her? Graham, or someone who was starting to look like an air brushed version of him, was taking unprecedented football trips away with 'the lads', none of whom she'd ever heard of before, and was buying her boxes of guilt chocolates, while inexplicably highlighting her favourite programmes in green ink. If he'd come downstairs in a leopard-skin thong with a packet of ribbed ticklers under his arm he couldn't have announced more clearly that he was having an affair. Except he wouldn't need the ribbed ticklers any more, she reminded herself, apart from … yuck! Apart from reasons of hygiene and the avoidance of STDs. And Charlotte – her daughter, indeed, but someone who became more of a mystery to her with each passing day, with each new hormone, and who took it for granted that she should have half of whatever was given to her mother as some sort of inalienable right – didn't have the courtesy to tell that same mother, the mother who'd given up – what, a career? Not exactly, perhaps, but the mother who'd given up, well, lots of things to be with her – that she'd now changed her name. Was that how she'd brought Charlotte up? Had she failed at the one job she'd been given permission to do? It was a sobering thought. She sank onto the sofa in a mood of mystified misery as the phone in her pocket trilled.

'Hu-o,' she mumbled through a very chewy chocolate caramel.

'Any luck on the babysitting front?' Ben sounded incredibly close by, and Bunty instantly ducked behind a cushion, dribbling toffee down the velour.

'No, sorry,' she said indistinctly.

'It's not your weekend, then?'

For a moment the arrogance of the man almost amused her. Okay, so she wasn't able to go out with him that weekend, but it wasn't like she didn't have a life without him, for goodness' sake. A girl – woman – could still have fun without a bronzed Kiwi in tow. But then she realised what he meant. Not her weekend. Her weekend of freedom while the ex took over the childcare. He meant that it wasn't her weekend *off*. 'No,' she said quickly. 'Not this weekend.'

'I understand,' said Ben, and Bunty's heart flowered again. Of course he did. He had kids. He was divorced, or separated, like her. Only she wasn't quite. He continued, 'Could you get away for an hour tomorrow? Lunch, maybe.'

'Oh! Well, I'll try. My daughter's bound to be at a friend's anyway.' If she'd thought faster, she could have made Graham take Charlotte with him. He kept saying it would be good for her to take up a sport.

'Great! How about the Pig and Cauli at one.'

What was it about that place? 'Or that wine bar we met in last time?'

Ben sounded disappointed. 'It's a bit fancy schmancy for lunch, don't you think? I fancy some good old fashioned tucker.'

'Okay,' said Bunty with a grin. 'See you at the P and C at one.'

She hung up quickly as Graham's bag nosed its way into the room. 'Right then, love, I'll be off.'

'I didn't hear a mini-bus,' she said, looking out at the empty street.

'Oh, we're meeting up at the squash club.' Graham dropped a kiss on the top of her head and backed out of the room quickly. 'See you tomorrow night.'

Bunty watched frostily as he reversed up the driveway, his wheels spitting out gravel on either side. Squash club. Right. Football. Yeah, right. Mini-bus to Coventry. Double, triple right. Did he think she was born yesterday? 'Well, du-uh,' she said in a surprisingly good impression of her daughter. Graham was so involved in his little tryst that he couldn't see how bloody obvious he was being. Obvious and a little bit pathetic. If Bunty hadn't been quite so mad with him, she could almost have sympathised. In a distinct grump, she squashed herself into the corner of the sofa with her battered box of Milk Tray, the remains of the bottle of Chablis and the remote control. Ant and Dec had better be good tonight, she thought.

Three hours later she woke up in a pool of chocolate drool, after a particularly lurid dream in which she was jelly-wrestling with Ant, then Dec, then both. What woke her up was Dec scrabbling to the edge of the jelly pool (which was, she was startled to note, Charlotte's old rubber paddling pool with various Disney characters in swimming trunks cavorting around the edge), and screaming, 'GET ME OUT OF HERE! GET ME OUT …'

'Mum,' said a voice in her left ear. 'Mum! You're shouting.'

Charlotte had removed the wine glass from her hand and was busy turning the volume down on the TV. 'You've slept through all your favourite programmes. Why don't you go to bed?'

'I … um … I think I might. What time is it?'

'Ten thirty,' said Charlotte, surfing through the channels until she landed on some sort of teen horror movie.

'Right,' said Bunty. She heaved herself out of the sofa, made sure the back door was locked and headed up the stairs. It wasn't until she had cleaned her teeth and put on her least sexy pyjamas (what was she on about – they were *all* the least sexy these days) that she realised what she'd overlooked.

She went back downstairs. 'Charlotte,' she said sharply.

'Hmmmm?' Her daughter barely looked up from the TV.

'Bed.'

'Aw, bu' Muu-uum …'

'I'm the mother. You're the child. Go to bed.'

Just in case, Bunty waited until Charlotte had trolled up the stairs before going up herself. Her life was twisted. They were having some *Freaky Friday* moment, where her routine and

Charlotte's were somehow reversed, where Graham had a new set of imaginary friends, and where she was trying to work out how to dispose of her daughter for an hour in the middle of a Sunday so she could go on a date.

Twisted.

Exciting. But twisted.

CHAPTER NINE

Pearl: So tell us, Bunty, when did you start to fall for Ben?

Bunty (*coyishly tucking hair behind ear*): Well, Pearl, I would probably have to say it was after our first lunch at the Pig and Cauli. He was very, very charming.

Finn: And your husband was behaving a little outrageously at this point?

Bunty: Absolutely. Pretending he was off to football matches when no such matches existed. Getting thinner and browner.

Pearl (*rolling her eyes in a co-conspirator fashion*): All of which just confirmed for you, after the vasectomy debacle, that he was having an affair.

Bunty (*sighing*): It did, Pearl. You know, I think I've been a good wife. I've done all the homemaking a woman could do. Our daughter was happy, well-rounded. But I suppose it just … just wasn't enough for Graham.

Finn (*to camera*): We're here talking to Bunty McKenna about her new book, *My Husband the Adulterer*.

Pearl: And it's a tale a lot of women, and possibly some men, will be more than able to relate to. Bunty, tell us why …

Bunty sat up in bed, brushing her dark fringe out of her eyes. Christ, ten o'clock. If Charlotte was any younger, there would have been a strong danger she could have burnt the house down by now. These days it was more than likely that Charlotte was still in her bedroom, either in bed, or lolling in front of the dressing table trying on stolen makeup (pilfered from Bunty or other friends' mums, not Boots the Chemist, although the way she was heading Bunty wouldn't absolutely swear that was the case).

Ten o'clock. Two hours to go until her clandestine meeting with Ben. Hence the interview dream, she supposed – her subconscious was paving the way for her forthcoming adultery. Had she been a good wife? Tick. Well, at least she had done all the things that good wives did: learnt to cook, produced dinner parties for bosses at the mere sniff of a raise or promotion, planned holidays and packed for them, washed and cleaned and polished and painted, injected a modicum of enthusiasm into the biweekly bedtime sports and never, ever strayed. That made her a good wife, didn't it? Or homemaker, as she was supposed to call it these days. Well, she'd made the home, and now Graham was breaking it. Her adultery was perfectly justified.

And Charlotte *was* happy and well-rounded, insomuch as she hadn't descended into the black-garbed depression and apparent drug-taking of the Emo or Goth (Charlotte had tried to explain the difference but it made no impression on Bunty, other than she was glad that Charlotte was not yet either). So she was a little harder to empathise with these days, what with her constant lugubrious lolling around the place and endless supply of facial quirks to denote that Bunty was a permanent embarrassment to her – she had actually said to Bunty recently, in tones of great seriousness, to 'like, never, ever speak in front of my friends again. In fact, if you didn't speak in public at all, like, ever, that would be really, really good.' All because Bunty had asked her friend (some strange vampiric girl called Jacinth, who to Bunty's untrained eye had definite Emo or Goth tendencies) if she'd like to stay for tea. Nobody did 'tea' any more apparently.

Anyway, at least she wasn't suicidal, self-harming, anorexic, bulimic, dating her teacher, meeting convicts in chat-rooms … Well, Bunty would have to keep an eye on that one, but it did seem that the worst thing that Charlotte was up to right now was a bit of giggly probing into inappropriate websites. Perhaps probing was the wrong word, thought Bunty with a wince. But it made her think of something.

Graham hadn't taken his laptop. Scampering out of bed, Bunty pulled the computer out from behind his chair, and booted it up as quickly as she could. The broadband connection was pretty instant; Graham had taken care of all the Wifi stuff – shame he didn't care so much about the wifey. Bunty tried a few of the topics that had appeared on the downstairs computer, but to no avail. In fact, when she looked at the things that popped up in place of the naughty words, Bunty wondered that anyone would find Graham interesting enough to have an affair with. No penises, but pension predictions. Not boobs, but bookings for Financial Strategies for Paupers. Viginas? Nothing. Even typing in 'vaginas' only brought up 'vagaries in the US dollar affects housing market'. Maybe he was having an affair with his job, thought Bunty viciously, trying to think up more rude words. He obviously adored it.

Her lexicon of lechery exhausted, Bunty went instead to the Chelsea site. It was very illuminating. 'Bastard,' she hissed. Not only were Chelsea not in the cup finals, they weren't even playing at Coventry. They'd played the previous day, at home. There was no way he was in a mini-bus with 'the lads' on his way to an away match. Well, not the football type, anyway.

'Right.' Bunty packed away the laptop, her crisis of conscience fully resolved. 'Shower.'

After a quick phone call to Kristiana to check she was available for a two hour lunchtime sit on Bunty's sofa watching the *Eastenders* omnibus, all expenses paid, Bunty launched herself into a full preparation for seduction. Not that it mattered whether she was shaven into alabaster smoothness today – there would be no sex for ages – but she wanted to be sure that when Ben swept her up into his arms, she would smell and feel and look so edible that he wouldn't be able to resist. He would clutch her tightly around the waist, lips parted slightly, the pupils of his eyes pulsating with love, their hearts pounding against each other like cartoon hearts with the knowledge, the anticipation, that this would be the first, the most perfect, the most fulfilling kiss of all time. A *Brief Encounter* kiss, heart-stopping, exquisitely painful. Love like it was on TV.

Half an hour later she trailed downstairs in a dress rather shorter than any she had worn for, well, the whole century, now that she thought of it. Charlotte looked up from her cornflakes, spoon paused en route. 'Where are we going?'

'You're not going anywhere,' said Bunty, parting her fringe this way and the other to see which way looked more seductive. Actually neither did. That was the only thing with short hair. It lay the way it was cut, and that was that. No swishing of the tresses from one side to the other, the parting undulating across the head while a swoop of hair hung sexily over one eye. Bunty's hair against the grain made her look like Tin-Tin. She gave up and pulled it forwards again with her fingers, suddenly realising that Charlotte was now eyeballing her with the utmost suspicion.

'Well, who's coming for lunch then?'

'Nobody. Well, Kristiana is coming to keep an eye on you. There's lasagne in the fridge and you can finish your science homework without my help, can't you, and …'

But Charlotte wasn't listening. 'Who's that then? Someone thinks they're coming for lunch.'

'Oh Jesus.'

Charlotte snorted. 'Mother. That is not Jesus.'

The figure striding across the gravel was dressed in a striped shirt, tight jeans and very cool Armani sunglasses. 'I didn't say Jesus,' said Bunty hastily. 'I said Jason.'

What the hell was he doing here? Bunty sprinted to the front door, hoping to head him off at the pass. 'What the hell are you doing here?' she asked, more directly.

Jason eyed her up and down like a prize cow and let out a filthy wolf-whistle. 'You scrub up nice. Were you expecting me? Oh, hello.'

This was to Charlotte, who had appeared in the hall in her cute but too small pyjama top and shorts. 'Hiya,' she said, spooning cornflakes into her mouth. Bunty winced again. When had Charlotte stopped being tongue-tied, mute in fact, in front of the opposite sex? First Daniel. Now Jason. She'd be introducing herself as Charlie next and inviting him in to view her laptop etchings.

'Charlotte! Back inside,' snapped Bunty, before turning her withering glance on Jason. 'How did you get my home address?'

'Followed you back the other night, didn't I.' It was a statement, not a question.

'That's appalling. How were you even allowed into this Croesus Club? No, don't tell me,' she added as an afterthought, seeing Jammy draw in a breath to impress her with his credentials. 'You have to go,' she said.

'But I've got a lunch date,' said Jason, clearly enjoying seeing her squirm.

'Jason, we have *not* got a lunch date.' Honestly, the cheek of the boy was quite astonishing.

'Not with you,' he said with a smirk, looking along the hall behind her.

'Oh. My. Christ.' But how? Charlotte must have been on the same website as her. She *was* meeting convicts in chat rooms. Even if Jason wasn't a prisoner yet, he was soon about to be. 'She's thirteen, you sick perv. What is it with you and age?'

At this, Jason at least had the grace to look a bit confused. A flush seeped along his greasy cheekbones. 'She told me she was twenty-five.'

'Twenty-five? Does she look twenty-five?'

Jason shrugged. 'Lot of people don't look their age these days. Do they, Bunty?'

This was horrible. Worse than horrible. Everything was sliding into a nightmarish, Technicolor horror-film. Any second now the doors and windows would all slam closed, and she and Charlotte would be left alone with this ghoul, this spotty, overprivileged axe-murdering stockbroker, and it was all her fault. She'd welcomed him into their lives. Agreed to meet him. Lied about herself. Tipped ice in his lap and then come straight home – of course he'd bloody well followed her. And then he'd peered in, rubbing his oily hands up and down his thighs and God only knew what else as he espied her baby, her little girl, and waited for Graham to be gone for him to carry out his master plan. Leering. Leaning over to shake her hand. *Let's think of it as a business venture. Two for the price of one. You, the old trollop, and her, the young floozy …*

Get out, she was about to scream. Get out, get away. She'd miss her date with Ben. Oh God, how could she even be thinking about dates with Ben. Dates with anyone. Look what a previous one had led to. But then his weasel head spun around at the sound of tyres on the gravel. 'Ah. Here she is,' he said.

Kristiana swivelled her long legs out of the door of her ancient Honda Civic. 'Ah. Jason. You made it.' She caught sight of Bunty in the doorway. 'It is all right with you, Bunty, yes? I met Jason after babysitting the other night. His car had broken down right outside! And I thought he could have lunch with Charlotte and I.'

'Charlotte and me,' corrected Bunty automatically. Of course, she thought crossly. Because correct grammar was really what mattered now.

'You are staying too?' Kristiana was understandably confused.

Bunty covered her face with her hands. 'No. Nobody is staying. At least, I'm going out, and Jason is leaving – not together! But I think you'll appreciate, Kristiana, that Charlotte is at an impressionable age, and Jason appears to be too, so I think it would be better if you met outside of my home, if you don't mind.'

Jason turned pink and then started to gesticulate to Kristiana. 'And don't think you can come back the minute my back's turned, Jason.' Did he think she was blind? Born yesterday? 'Kristiana, can I trust you on this? Because if I can't you'd better say now, and you can find someone else to babysit for in future.' She resisted the temptation to add 'Jason, perhaps.'

It was Kristiana's turn to go red. It was all Bunty could do not to sneer in Jason's face. Business deals? She could teach him a thing or two. There was no way Kristiana would take him over Bunty – a higher-than-average pay rate to mind a child who was hardly a child any more meant far more to a struggling student than the odd flash dinner. Kristiana stuttered, her English coming slightly unglued. 'Of coarseness. I would not dream to make Charlotte imp ... impressioned. Jason,' she added primly, 'I will give you text. Tomorrow.'

'All right,' said Jason eventually. He'd clearly been outmanoeuvred, and he looked at Bunty with even more lascivious respect than he had the other night. With a sweep of a pointed finger at Bunty, which she took to mean 'I might be shagging the help but you are hot, baby', he slimed his way back across the gravel, clambered into Jammy the Golf and roared off.

'I am sorry, Bunty,' said Kristiana, looking genuinely contrite. 'I did not think ...'

'It's okay. I was young once, you know,' replied Bunty. Young? Once? Young and dating and 'I remember what its like'? The hypocrisy of the situation made her want to laugh really. She'd stopped the babysitter having a date because she, mother of the babysittee, and married at that, was off on an illicit date herself. Oh yes. I'm such a good mother, Pearl. The best. Salt of the earth. Maldon bloody sea salt at that.

They were still on the doorstep, so Bunty stood back to let Kristiana in, checking her watch. She followed Kristiana into the lounge. 'Charlotte needs to get dressed and do her science homework. There's lasagne in the fridge if you're hungry, and I'll ... I'd best be going.'

Now that it actually came to it, her earlier fervour for her date had somewhat dissipated. What did she think she was doing? These dates were highly unreliable. How on earth did Graham stand it? He had to be in constant fear of his mistress turning up at the door, or calling Bunty and screaming at her down the phone for not appreciating him, not loving him like she did, not giving him the mind-blowing sex that they were having, right now, in the back of a mini-bus on the M6.

'I won't be long,' she said finally to her daughter and her daughter's minder, who were both staring at her with a sort of vapid curiosity as she struggled with her conscience in the lounge doorway.

It made her all the more determined. She wouldn't be long. Just long enough to tell Ben that this was all a mistake, that even if her husband was a philandering pig she didn't have the right makeup to go finding a new model behind his back; that there had to be some other alternative for her to being thrown out on the street with a couple of black bin liners and her Spandeau Ballet CD collection. 'I'll just be an hour.'

But then she saw him, stacking beer mats in a quiet corner of the Pig and Cauli, clearly as nervous as she was, and her resolve melted again. 'I can't stay long,' she said the moment she arrived at the table.

Ben had half-stood, probably intending to give her a kiss on the cheek, or possibly some kind of Maori rubbing-noses kind of greeting, but Bunty's words took the wind straight out of his sails. He hovered uncertainly for a moment in a Neanderthal crouch and then plumped back down into his seat. 'Oh,' he said. 'Well, you did say you wouldn't be able to.'

'And I meant it,' said Bunty, more fiercely than she intended.

Ben spread his hands defensively. 'Okay.'

'Oh God, I'm sorry.' Bunty pulled out a chair and sank down opposite him. 'I just had a run-in with the babysitter and I feel a bit … a bit strange being out at this time of the day.'

'It's just lunchtime,' said Ben softly, but she could see by the tilt of his head that he understood. It felt strange for him too. Strange, but nice.

'I know.' She picked up a menu cheerfully. 'So are we eating?'

Ben coloured slightly, his tan becoming more pronounced. 'Well, sure. Or we could just get a drink. Or we could get a drink, and … and room service.'

'Room service?' Bunty put down the menu, perplexed. Then she looked out of the window. So that was why the Pig and Cauli was so popular with these dating guys. It was one of those inn-type pubs with a Travel Lodge attached. What was actually on the menu was … her.

Ben watched her face carefully and then shook his head. 'Sorry. Sorry, I shouldn't have even suggested it.'

'No, no … but you're not on your yacht?'

'I thought I'd get on some solid ground for the weekend. I stayed here last night. I didn't … Oh God, you think I just booked the room for lunch?' Ben groaned so loudly that the party of six on the next table all looked up at them.

Bunty leaned in. 'It did sound a bit 'by the hour', if you know what I mean.'

Ben slid his hand across the table and grabbed her fingers. 'I'm so sorry, Bunty. You're a lovely lady, and you must think I'm some bloody crass Antipodean who's only after one thing. I really did invite you for lunch. Food only.'

But the sip of wine, the strange Jason moment, the knowledge that Graham was doing the same thing somewhere else, and the electric jangle of Ben's touch … Suddenly Bunty found herself picking up the card key from under the stack of beer mats. 'I'm suddenly not hungry,' she said.

'You're going?'

She smiled in what she hoped was a seductive manner but which she suspected came across rather like a ventriloquist's dummy. 'Only to your room. What number?'

Together, both slightly dazed, they made their way through the maze of tables and out into the sunshine. Ben stopped her on the threshold of Room 13. 'I don't want to rush you, Bunty. Are you sure you're ready?'

No, she wasn't sure. She wasn't sure at all. But then, how could she have prepared herself for this type of occasion? She couldn't do rehearsals. Dry runs. There was nothing for it but to jump straight in. Like Graham had done.

'There's just one thing,' she said. 'You have to kiss me first.'

So he did, cupping her head in his enormous hand, pausing, a tiny look of concern in his eyes that was so endearingly sweet, before he lowered his lips to hers, and the soundtrack of *From Here to Eternity* came to life somewhere under her eyelids as they fluttered closed.

CHAPTER TEN

'Just remind me again why we're here.' Kat squinted at the sun that was just about making an appearance over the horizon. 'It's bloody freezing.'

Bunty hopped from one foot to the other. Maybe Lycra cycling shorts were not the right attire for a dawn meeting on a Wednesday, but she hadn't been absolutely sure what the right attire would be. A green costume? Something Maid Marian-ish?

'I told you,' she said, her breath coming out in puffs, 'I told Ben that this is the kind of stuff I do. Or at least that's what he took it to mean. I have to try and impress him somehow.'

They lined up behind the ten metre line as instructed, Kat slapping her hands together to keep herself warm. 'But I thought you told him you liked fencing. And I know you meant the woody stuff, not lots of lunging and thrusting like he thought, but this, my darling, is archery. Ar-che-ry.'

Bunty ignored how much Kat sounded like Charlotte, spelling things out for her as if she were some kind of idiot. Fair enough. Perhaps she was some kind of idiot. In fact, there was no 'perhaps' about it. Anyone who had had a gorgeous All Black look-alike trapped in a Traveller's Lodge and completely at their mercy – an All Black who had just delivered a heart-stopping snog right on the very threshold and who was clearly eager to seal the deal, as it were – and who had then completely refused to go through with it, was actually incapable of going through with it … Well, that person had to be an idiot, right?

It had all seemed so easy, when he removed his tongue from her mouth, dragged his teeth across her lower lip, and looked down into her eyes with just a hint of panting going on beneath his polo shirt. For her part, Bunty suspected she was actively dribbling. The kiss was delicious. He was delicious. And this, behind the door, when he'd fumbled with the key and staggered inside with his arm around her shoulders, was going to be just delicious too. But somehow, when he had her pinned against the back of the door with an exploratory hand sliding up her skirt, she had developed an attack of hysteria. She'd actually laughed right down his throat. It was a wonder she hadn't given him the bends.

'Oh, I'm sorry, I'm sorry,' she gasped, leaning her head on his chest as another wave of giggles swept over her. 'I don't know what came over me.'

'Well, it wasn't me,' said Ben, which just set her off again.

'No, no, I'm really sorry, it's just that … it's just that …'

'My kissing's abysmal,' he finished for her.

'No! Really, it's lovely, but … ha …'

Ben leaned a hand on the door, starting to laugh himself. 'So I shouldn't be offended?'

'Oh, please don't, don't be offended.' Bunty wiped a tear from her eye and shook herself down. 'It's just that …'

Just what, exactly? That she'd suddenly remembered she had a husband at home? Well, not at home exactly, but somewhere around. That she'd found herself looking over Ben's shoulder and noticing that his bag was on the bed and wasn't even opened, so he really had booked the room that day, possibly by the hour?

That it was broad daylight outside, and across the pathway grannies and their grandkids were tucking into a nice carvery lunch with overcooked sprouts? Or that she'd had the opportunity to think, as his hand slid up her thigh, that she'd dressed like she was expecting this – sex; a quickie – and hadn't she promised herself that the way to bag a Ben was to avoid exactly this situation? It was all of those things, but it boiled down to one inevitable conclusion: the whole thing was bloody ridiculous. She, Bunty McKenna, was bloody ridiculous. Bloody … ha … ha ha … ridiculous.

She'd finally gathered enough breath to speak. 'I can't do this, Ben. I'm sorry.'

'Me too,' said Ben, but with a wry quirk of the lips which at least showed that he wasn't angry. She couldn't have stood that too. 'First time?'

First time? She was thirty-eight and married with a child, for Chrissakes. No 'nearly forty-year-old virgins' here. 'Oh. First time since my marriage … She faltered. Well, yes.'

Ben nodded sympathetically, and gave her shoulders a squeeze. He didn't, she noticed, mention that it was his first time too. But then he was properly separated. He was perfectly within his rights to have slept with other women since his marriage ended, before meeting Bunty. Graham hadn't even waited for the separation before hopping onto the gym bunny.

Instead of speaking, Ben leaned in for another kiss. 'I like you, Bunty. You're … unusual.'

In other words, he thinks I'm a freak, she thought. She smoothed down her skirt. 'I think I'd better go home.'

At which Ben had nodded regretfully and held open the door. 'I'll call you,' he said. 'Tomorrow.'

The death knell. I'll call you. Bunty threw herself into the Mini, almost tempted to turn around and go give him something to remember her by, so that he actually would call her. Adam had been especially good at the 'I'll call you'. The one that meant 'I'll wait until I haven't got anyone else lined up and then I'll call you' or 'I need money so I'll call you' or, occasionally, 'I have just remembered we're supposed to be in a relationship and I feel really bad that I've not acknowledged your existence for five days straight so I'll offer you this little bone and … call you'.

Oh yes. She knew all about 'I'll call you'. That was the last she would hear from Ben.

She'd driven home despondently, hardly registering that Graham was jumping out of a powder-blue Mondeo in front of her, not a mini-bus at all, and was waving goodbye to the driver who she couldn't really see but seemed to be tall with short dark hair, or that Jason was parked down the street waiting for Kristiana. I'll call you. I'm sorry, I'm bloody ridiculous. You're unusual. I'll call you. The whole scene played over and over in her head until it was picked so full of holes it could have made a doily.

'I'll call you!' shouted Graham to the pale blue Mondeo.

'You twat,' she muttered, loudly enough for him to almost hear as she stalked past him on the drive. How dare he? She almost had a moment of sympathy for his lover. The tart would never hear from Graham now, that was for sure.

'What?' Graham dropped his bag on the drive. Bunty resisted the temptation to kick it. A shag bag. Rather like Ben's, although she didn't like to draw the comparison. Did all men have them? Were they all ready packed, like women's cases ready for the hospital when they were about to give birth? Though Bunty doubted that the contents of Graham's bag ran to size 0 baby clothes and a pack of super absorbent sanitary pads.

Graham picked up the bag and followed Bunty inside. 'Did you just call me a twat?'

'Why would I do that?' said Bunty with a hollow laugh.

'I don't know ….'

'How about the fact that Chelsea weren't even playing today? And if they had been playing the match wouldn't that have been happening right now?'

Graham faltered and then turned pink. 'I … I got it wrong. That's why we're back early. Ryan just dropped me off.'

And just for a moment, Bunty felt her lip wobble. 'Graham, forgive me if I don't believe you.' Not giving him a chance to respond, she stalked into the kitchen.

Amazingly, for some many reasons, at that moment her mobile phone had rung and a deep voice said, 'Told you I'd call you.'

'Oh! Hi … I … just got in.'

She could hear the smile in Ben's voice. 'Thought I'd better make sure you got home okay. Didn't laugh yourself off the road or anything.'

Bunty looked at Graham, still standing flustered in the hallway, then checking in on Charlotte. 'No. No more laughing.'

At this, Ben laughed himself. 'Okay. Well, make yourself a cup of tea,' he said in an excruciating fake English accent, 'and I'll call you tomorrow. If that's okay.'

'That's just fine,' said Bunty warmly.

Actually, he hadn't called the next day, but he'd called early the morning after that to say he was out on the boat. 'Maybe you could join me for lunch?'

'Can't, sorry. I promised my neighbour I'd help re-bury her cat.'

Ben paused. 'You could just say you're washing your hair.'

'No, it's true! I wouldn't make that up!' said Bunty, kicking herself. Everything she did or said seemed to convince Ben even more that she wasn't interested in seeing him. Time to turn the tables. 'Tomorrow? I could bring a picnic.'

It was Ben's turn to sound contrite. 'Sorry, I'm out on the yacht for the next couple of days. But I tell you what, you're a good outdoorsy girl, aren't you?'

'Yeah!' carolled Bunty, lying her head off. The most outdoorsy she'd been recently was belly-crawling through the drainage system in her own back garden, or carrying her shopping across Tesco's car park.

'Well, how about meeting up on Saturday for some fresh air. No bedrooms involved, I promise.'

'Great!'

'So you'll find something for us to do, seeing as you're the local? Ask your fencing mates or whatever.'

'Sure!'

'Call you tomorrow.'

'Right! Bye!'

Bunty had put the phone down, exhausted from having to speak in such an enthusiastic, exclamatory way before she'd even had chance to make the beds. And then she'd set to with the Yellow Pages, finding something in which she could become proficient in half a week, at least enough to impress Ben with her outdoorsyness.

Which was how she and Kat, dragooned in for moral support, found themselves at an archery lesson at 6.30 a.m. on a damp Wednesday. (Or perhaps it was always damp at dawn. Bunty didn't usually see it.) If she played her cards right she could have three lessons by Saturday, and practice a bit in between times, maybe taking pot shots at Graham, and by the time of meeting Ben on Saturday afternoon (with Graham *actually* at football, and Charlotte at orchestra rehearsal with her oboe) she could wow him by her expertise with a bow.

'It's your turn.' Kat shoved her from behind. 'That way!'

Spun around by her friend, Bunty eyed the target. Surely it had got further away? 'Right,' the instructor was bellowing, 'now draw that back till your hand is under your jaw and the string's pressing on your nose …'

'My what?' Bunty turned to look at the instructor, and immediately let go of the taut string. It twanged against her lower left arm like a cat-o'-nine-tails. Bunty yowled.

'Didn't you have your arm guard on?' The female instructor hurried over. 'It was the first thing we covered this morning. People! Very important to wear your arm guard, or you'll end up like Binty here.'

106

'Bunty.' The pain was excruciating, and before her eyes a welt was rising on the white skin of her underarm like some sort of Masonic insignia, while the bloom of a new bruise brushed the rest of it.

'Arm guard on. Onward and upward. Aim and … good!' The instructor watched Bunty's arrow sail over the target and pulled Kat forward into her place. 'Very close. You next.'

Somehow Kat turned out to be a natural, getting two bull's-eyes out of five shots while Bunty was lucky to hit the target. 'It's only cos you're so little,' said Kat. 'I've got arms like a shot-putter so I can pull the stringy thing back more easily.' She loosed another arrow off across the patchy grass and it thunked solidly into the gold area of the target. 'See. I love it. It's the only sport I've ever been able to do.'

Bunty sighed. 'I'm not sure it counts as a sport. That's why I chose it.'

Neither she, Kat, nor Cally had ever been into any kind of sporting activity really. The closest they'd got was paint-balling on a Saturday afternoon, and that had stopped early because Bunty bruised too easily. There was the evidence again, spreading up her arm like yellow fever. She'd tried archery once before, at one of Graham's corporate events, where they'd been in a team with some tall, dark, geeky kind of guy from Acquisitions. His kindly wife who'd been so bad at everything that Bunty had looked like a trained athlete by comparison. Who were they? Petra and someone. Brian? Or … Ryan. Shit! Maybe there was a Ryan, after all.

'Course it counts as a sport,' said Kat, drawing her hand back to her chin like a professional, practically slicing her nose in two with the string. Ah. The instructor had been right, after all. 'They do it at the Olympics, don't they? So it must be a proper sport.'

'Yeah, like beach volleyball,' scoffed Bunty. 'And that weird walking with your bum stuck out. And sailing ... damn!'

Sailing. Of course! She would have had a chance for at least a couple of sailing lessons, and then she could have thoroughly impressed Ben with her expertise and jargon while they shot round the Isle of Wight on his yacht with champagne in their free hand – the one they weren't using to caress the other's cheek.

But sailing wasn't a possibility right now, so archery it was – anything to try to convince Ben, who had showered her with ten days of phone attention, all at the right times when Graham wouldn't get suspicious and all solicitous, sweet, funny phone calls that made Bunty squirm with glee. It was like being a teenager again, only without pimples. And, okay, with a husband and child in their place.

By Saturday morning, however, she'd given up altogether on archery. Even Kat's enthusiasm had palled, since the third lesson of the week had them standing behind the twenty-five metre line so that Kat's laser-straight arrows no longer hit the target every time. 'I'm getting worse,' she complained. 'I thought lessons were supposed to help you to get better.'

Bunty nodded. She'd given up even collecting her arrows now and was just loitering around behind Kat, letting the pale sunlight freckle her face. 'Like me with tennis. I started out really well. Francois was even going to put me in the intermediate group. And then the more I learned, the more pathetic I got.'

'You did,' said Kat kindly. 'You were really only ball-girl material by the end of that course.'

'Thanks.' It was true, but harsh to hear it none the less. Her last few lessons had been laughable. 'Oh God. What if it's the same with all physical activities?'

Kat guffawed, sending her arrow wonkily through the air so it hit next door's target. 'What, do you mean sex?'

'Don't laugh! Maybe that's why I couldn't do it last week.' Bunty remembered the scene, appalled. 'Perhaps I've done it too much and learned more, and now I'm thinking about it too hard, and technique and all that, and maybe I'm just really crap at it now.' In a crazed way it made sense. She had the distinct feeling that she had been much better at it with Adam when she knew nothing, and in the early days of Graham when he knew nothing, than in the current frame of watching TV sex and knowing that everyone these days had to be a professionally trained lap dancer and amateur porn star to ensnare anyone in the bedroom department.

'Well, I haven't done it for about a year,' said Kat, prodding her with the feathered end of an arrow. Even that hurt. 'I must be bloody excellent again by now.'

'Poor Simon,' said Bunty with a grin.

'I know! Three weeks and counting.' Kat couldn't have looked more pleased with the prospect. 'Anyway, I wouldn't worry about it. Ben's obviously dead keen. And the only reason you couldn't do anything last week was because you were feeling guilty.'

'I was.'

'I tell you what,' said Kat with a distinct gleam in her eye. 'Why don't you surprise him this afternoon and book a room somewhere yourself? After all, your shagging ability has got to be better than your archery.'

There was a warped logic to her friend's idea, thought Bunty, as she shoved lunch dishes into the dishwasher a few hours later. What was blatantly evident was that she wasn't going to be able to impress Ben with her sporting prowess. And she'd left it too late to cook up some delicious spread and get to him through his stomach. Plus, now she thought about it, she hadn't had sex for several months now. Perhaps she was a novice all over again. She might even be really, really good at it.

Just to stand her in good stead, after she'd flicked a desultory hand at Graham dropping Charlotte at orchestra on his way to the match (she thought about trailing him but was too excited by the prospect of her own date), she sprayed Chanel No 5 behind her knees, then instantly regretted it. Was Chanel too old fashioned? Old, even? Perhaps she ought to raid Charlotte's dressing table for Eau de Britney or 'Pink' by Pink, or whatever the latest scent was. But then she'd have to shower to get the Chanel off, or spray Pink somewhere else like a patch test, and then she'd smell like a perfume department, or worse, like some Tawdry Audrey in a saloon scene … and anyway, there wasn't time. Chanel smelt nice. That would have to do.

Bunty put on her best underwear, then her best casual-and-not-trying-too-hard summer dress, and an extra squirt of No 5 across her belly, just for good luck. Then, grabbing the box of Marks & Spencers nibbles, a plaid rug and a bottle of vintage cava (a casual-and-not-trying-too-hard champagne), she headed out to the Mini, then on to the park-like grounds of the hotel they'd agreed on. At the perfect moment she could let him know there was a suite booked in her name. He'd be able to stay in it all night, if he wanted. After.

She could hardly wait.

To: admin@Croesusclub.com

From: buntymckenna@ntsworld.com

Hi! Priscilla! Me again.

Just wondering if you could let me have Ben's mobile number. Again. I can't seem to find it on my mobile although we have spoken so, so often. Only he didn't turn up for a date and I really need to contact him.

How are you, by the way?

Bunty x

To: buntymckenna@ntsworld.com

From: admin@croesusclub.com

Hello Bunty, I am well, thank you for your concern.

Unfortunately we only give out our ladies' numbers to the gentlemen who express an interest, and it is up to them to make contact. You'll appreciate that it is mainly, though not exclusively, the gentleman who are the 'breadwinners' and targeted members, and if any of them do not choose to stay in touch after their dates, then that is their prerogative.

Shall we move on to a third candidate for you? There is another gentleman on the books who has expressed an interest in meeting with you.

Yours,

Priscilla

To: admin@croesusclub.com

From: buntymckenna@ntsworld.com

Hi, P, no, I don't think you get it. Ben and I were in constant contact, it's just that his phone must be a New Zealand one or something because the number doesn't come up on my mobile. And I'm worried about him! Suppose he's drowned or something? I know he would have turned up to our date. It was all arranged and we'd spoken about it every day for the previous ten.

Just his number? Please, Priscilla? And then I'm sure we'll all find that we don't need to bother with a third candidate. You can even charge your Love Lottery fee!

Bun x

To: buntymckenna@ntsworld.com

From: admin@croesusclub.com

Dear Bunty,

You don't think he was blocking his calls, and then didn't turn up deliberately? It's just one theory.

Yours,

Priscilla

To: admin@croesusclub.com

From: buntymckenna@ntsworld.com

Ouch, Priscilla. No, I don't think that. Or at least, I didn't.

No, I'm genuinely concerned. He may be in need of help. Rolled up in a sail and hoisted half way up a mast. Trapped under a barrel of rum. I'm sure I saw something like that on Howard's Way once.

Just one little call?

B x

To: buntymckenna@ntsworld.com

From: admin@croesusclub.com

Fine. Just to be sure that Ben is indeed not incapacitated in some way, I will make contact with him and make sure he is okay.

I'll confirm as soon as I hear, but I would point out that we cannot operate as go-betweens once dates have been established, nor am I a nursemaid. If he just doesn't want to get in touch, there's very little I can do.

Yours,

Priscilla

PS. Do let me know if you reconsider on that third date option. Mallory is very keen!

To: admin@croesusclub.com

From: buntymckenna@ntsworld.com

Okay, well over a week now. I suppose I could give Mallory a try.

Bunty

CHAPTER ELEVEN

Waiting for Ben had been bad enough. Realising that he wasn't going to be in contact again, after a whole week of pacing, hand-rubbing waiting, was like having teeth pulled without anaesthetic. Although she had sworn she would not and had even promised Kat that she wouldn't do these things, Bunty had engaged in several activities that would have made Jammy Jason proud and that bordered, in fact, on stalking. This included calling back any unidentified person who had rung her mobile in the last three weeks, even people for whom the date of the call came slightly before she had ever met Ben. (He'd called earlier to set up their date, hadn't he?) Consequently she'd had several confused, ill-prepared conversations. 'Dan, Dan the Drainage Man', who was waiting for a pump, thought she'd rung to hassle him. Mary, who was waiting for Dan to turn up with the pump, thought she'd rung to hassle her. And when she got the instructor from archery all Bunty could think of to say was, 'Oh! Hi. I had to tell you how much I'm enjoying the course. It's fabulous.'

'But you haven't been for the last five sessions.'

'I'm … I'm just nursing an injury but I'll be back very soon.'

'Well, the next course starts a week on Saturday and will be another 120.'

'Fine! See you there! Great!'

One very disturbing conversation was with Ryan from Graham's work. On hearing a man's voice she'd thought with a leap of her heart it was Ben. Then she realised with disappointment that the unidentified number on the same Saturday as she'd been waiting for Ben to picnic with her (or on her, whatever he fancied) was Graham using Ryan's phone and calling from the match he was genuinely attending to tell her he'd be late home. And now she'd put herself through it twice, first on the day itself, when of course she'd failed to pick up Charlotte in time and had been in trouble from all quarters while trying to bite back her own anxiety at the lack of Ben, and secondly when she responded to a deep 'Hello,' with 'Hi stranger!' in what she hoped was a breezy, sexy voice.

'Who's that?' the man had said cautiously, and Bunty realised instantly that it was an English accent on the end.

She'd laughed airily, saying 'Who's that yourself. It's Bunty, of course,' while racking her brains trying to think who it could be on the other end.

'Graham's wife Bunty?'

'Yep! Surprise, huh?' Graham's wife Bunty. It had to be someone from work. Nobody else would put Graham's name before hers. Who the hell could it be?

The voice sounded half-pleased, half-surprised. 'Very much so. Haven't seen you since that corporate activity day.'

Oh Jesus. Now it came back to her in all its glory. Ryan and Petra. The most boring couple in the world. There really was a Ryan. And hadn't he … hadn't he … Oh God. He'd flirted with her, in his disgusting 'I'm-such-an-outgoing-actuary-I'll look-at-your-shoes instead-of-my-own-when-I'm-talking-to-you and perving at her ankles' kind of a way. So that was who Graham was using as his alibi. Was that the best he could do?

Anyway, now she was stuck with him. She'd rung on his private number, and from the sound of it he was more than a little pleased to hear from her. 'I heard things weren't going too well, you know, between you and Graham,' said Ryan conspiratorially. 'I'm always …. available … if you want to talk.'

So that's what he'd heard, was it? And now he was offering a shoulder to cry on. Bunty nearly gagged. 'No, no, nothing like that! I just thought, well, we've not seen you in so long, I was wondering if you and Petra would like to come to dinner? Soon.'

'Oh. Oh, yes! We'd love to. When were you thinking?'

'Well, I just have to get Graham's dates off him, seeing as he's so busy with … with football, and I'll get right back to you. Bye.'

And she'd belted the 'end call' button, not quite sure which was creating the bile in her stomach – her loathing for Ryan, or her self-loathing for the scheming cow this whole thing had turned her into.

Not that it stopped her in her new role as stalker supreme, driving several times a day past the Pig and Cauli, and the wine bar where they'd first met, in the hope of spotting Ben (although what she would have done had she seen him, she wasn't quite sure, especially as it seemed eminently possible that he could be with someone else). She'd even spent an afternoon at the local marina, which wasn't actually that local at all, trying to see which yachts looked most like a Kiwi yacht, after first establishing which boats looked most like yachts.

It was only when she'd agreed to have a glass of wine with Kat and insisted on meeting at 'their' wine bar that she finally spotted the error of her ways. Kat patted her hand. 'He's gone, love.'

'But what if he's not? What if he's still here?' Bunty could feel her neck getting blotchy and hot.

Kat shrugged. 'It doesn't matter. Whether he's here right now, in this very bar, the facts are that one, he stood you up; two, he hasn't called you in ten days; and three, you're looking far too skinny so you obviously haven't eaten in a week and it's not fair that he should be doing that to you when you barely even know the guy.'

Bunty sipped her wine thoughtfully. All that Kat said was correct, factually, but that didn't stop her from feeling that they should have had something very special going on between them. There'd been the instant attraction, the assiduous attention, the kiss … Oh, that kiss!

'… Graham?' Kat was saying.

'What? Sorry.'

'I was asking,' said Kat patiently, 'how Graham's been behaving recently. Do you still think he's having an affair?'

Bunty flushed. 'I'm sure of it. I just happened to be driving past the squash club the other afternoon and – '

'Which just happens to be near the Pig and Cauli,' said Kat.

'And anyway, there was Graham, getting out of bloody Ryan's car – who I now have to have dinner with, by the way – and kissing that same blonde woman. '

'The one with the small tight bottom?'

'How many blondes are there?'

'I'm blonde,' said Kat, reasonably. 'But I don't have a small tight bottom.'

'Anyway,' said Bunty, now thoroughly depressed. 'Graham is clearly having an affair with Kylie Minogue, and the person I thought I was about to be having an affair with, leading to marriage and my get-out clause from Graham and his second family, has done a runner. Gone. Vanished.'

The reality finally hit her. She'd sat like an idiot, spread out on her plaid blanket weaving her daisy chain in what she hoped would be a picture of bucolic loveliness, waiting for him to stride around the corner in Byronic perfection and whisk her away to his yacht like some long-gone episode of *Poldark*. And he hadn't even called with an excuse. 'He's gone,' she whispered.

'I know,' said Kat slowly, and she filled up Bunty's glass with an empathy bordering on reverence.

Bunty sighed, as much for Kat as for herself. 'God, this is what it's like for you all the time, isn't it? Waiting for a call, hoping something will come of a chance meeting, wondering why the man who was so lovely to you yesterday has forgotten you exist today.'

'It's called 'being single', my friend.' Kat clinked her glass against Bunty's. 'Welcome to my world. No, I mean it, you're welcome to it. He may be twelve thousand miles away, but at least I now have Simon.'

'I need a Simon,' wailed Bunty, the third glass of wine starting to turn her red neck even redder.

Kat scowled, a sign that she was thinking very hard. 'That's what's weird,' she said. 'I thought you had one. A Simon, I mean.'

'With Ben?'

'No. With Graham. I mean, he had to have been a bit Simonish. Otherwise I couldn't have seen any other reason why you'd be with him. He's so … so not an Adam.'

It was a pivotal moment. Bunty slumped back in her chair, defeated. God, Kat was probably right. She'd *had* a Simon – a steadfast, constant sort of a person who, from what she could glean from Kat and from Cally, liked being a provider, liked the old-fashioned approach to life. Her own Simon didn't, sadly, have the stomach of a Greek statue as Simon was rumoured to possess, although … hadn't she seen what might be the beginning of a muscle when Graham had got out of the shower that morning? 'It doeshn't matter,' she slurred out of nowhere, startling Kat who had not really been waiting for her to respond. 'I had a Shimon, and he's sh … shagging Kylie. And I had a Ben, but he's disapproved. I mean, disappeared. I need a … a new man,' and she thumped the table to underline the point, scattering Bombay mix in all directions.

'Good.' Kat nodded approvingly. 'See, if that were me, I'd have had the 'all men are bastards' discussion for two weeks, then eaten myself silly for another month, then gone into hibernation for maybe two years. You are so …' She searched for the word. 'So man-wise.'

'I think like a man?'

Kat surged forward, her breasts spilling over the table like an unrestrained duvet. 'No. Yes. You are wise to men. And to be wise to men, you have to think like one. Don't be like me … all chocolate-eating and sorry for yourself. No! You have to move on. Get the next one. Find a new man. Forget Simons and Bens. Who needs 'em? Go and find a … a good one!'

'I bloody will!' shouted Bunty, slapping the table again.

There and then, while Kat blearily texted Simon as he got up that same morning on the other side of the world, Bunty sent an email from the newfangled phone slash movie theatre slash personal computer that Graham had insisted on her having, even though she only knew how two of the functions worked.

'I just dumped Simon,' said Kat proudly.

'Oh.' Bunty frowned. That wasn't quite how this was meant to go, was it? 'Is he upset?'

Kat peered at the tiny screen on her phone. 'No, he says, 'All right, lovely, why don't you have a sleep and text me in the morning. Love you, Simon.''

'He doesn't sound very dumped.'

'Nah, I'm always doing it,' said Kat, wrinkling her nose with delicious thoughts of Simon. 'He really gets me, you know?'

So this was what it was going to be like, thought Bunty, shaking her head in wonderment and not a little fear. Having to find someone who really 'got' her. Dumping people when you didn't mean it just to find out how much they really wanted you. Playing games. Not turning up to dates. Disappearing just when the other person was hooked.

Right at that moment, she'd been ready for it. Bring it on, she thought. Man number three from the Croesus Club.

Now that she was actually waiting for Mallory (sexy voice, posh, rather Nigel Havers-ish), parked in a corner of the lounge bar of the very same hotel she had booked in her seduction plan for Ben, Bunty was rather less sure of what she doing. She had to prepare herself for her husband's imminent departure. For one thing. Graham's behaviour was ever more erratic and bizarre. Having been delighted that Bunty had arranged dinner with Ryan and Petra ('I didn't think you even liked them. Great! Great to be doing something together.'), he had now taken to lurking behind the letterbox, practically wrestling the letters from the postwoman's hand as she fed them through the slot. Bunty was almost enjoying his discomfort.

'What are you waiting for now? The bill for your hair plugs? More indicting Visa statements?'

Graham laughed, a peculiar high-pitched keening. 'Ha! Ha, funny. Funny Bunny, that's you. No, just … just expecting Ryan's acceptance to dinner.'

'Very formal,' said Bunty, 'writing and so on. Most people just text these days.'

Graham nodded slowly. 'Well, that's Ryan. He is very formal.'

Bunty had just shrugged. She didn't honestly care any more, about Ryan, or the forthcoming dinner, or Graham and his prevaricating. She was moving on. Man-wise, like Kat said. Waiting for her third man.

The third man, thought Bunty, glancing at her watch. At least she had become a little more man-wise, or certainly date-wise. This time she'd suggested coffee, morning coffee, in a very lovely lounge from which she could make an early escape and would surely not be expected to drink champagne or anything else alcoholic, or slip off to a waiting bedroom. She'd also made sure, through Priscilla, that Mallory was seriously looking for a new wife, wasn't just out of a relationship, and wasn't masquerading as his own father. No, Priscilla had assured her, Mallory was a very trustworthy client, widowed early, keen to settle down again, and was definitely old enough to date without a chaperone. Things were looking good for the third man, even though deep down Bunty knew he wouldn't be able to win her over as ably as the second man had. Plus, he might have children. Little children if he'd been widowed early. Was she ready to take on someone else's kids? She had enough trouble with her own. Trying not to jump her head too far into the future, Bunty sipped her coffee in its dainty china cup. The third man. Orson Welles sprang into her head. Ding de ding de dinggggg, de dinggggggg. Ding de ding de dingggg, de dinggggg …

'Bunty, hello, what a lovely setting you've chosen.'

Christ, it is Orson Welles, thought Bunty, smiling up at the man who'd appeared from behind her chair. Orson Welles as he would be now if he were alive. Was he still alive? Anyway, he'd be about a hundred and sort of a caved-in mountain of a man like Mallory before her. Or was she thinking of Hemingway? In Bunty's mind they were always one and the same person. Why was that?

All these thoughts and more zipped through her brain as she tried to stand to greet her 'date' but found herself trapped on one side by his walking stick – his bloody *walking stick* – which at least wasn't a zimmer but was definitely much needed as Mallory heaved his withered bulk into the chair opposite her with the assistance of a passing waiter.

'You look shocked.' Mallory smiled winsomely at Bunty, and she was simultaneously pleased and horrified to note that his teeth were small, white and even, meaning that while they weren't the tumbledown, acid-yellow gravestones of some elderly mouths, they were most definitely false. Come out at night false. Pucker at the lips in the hope of a gummy snog while the teeth are in a glass false. 'Is it my stick? Priscilla was meant to tell you that I'm marginally disabled. Not too much, nothing that matters, if you know what I mean,' he wheezed, 'but enough to get me one of those nifty little stickers for my car. Park anywhere, Mallory can.'

Bunty recovered slightly, trying not to speak to him as she would her own grandfather, had he been alive. 'No! Are you comfortable there? We could sit you somewhere else …'

Oh God, she *was* talking to him as if he were her grandfather, or another dusty object that could be plonked somewhere different for a better view. But if she sat him somewhere else, she could run – run, as fast as her nimble, not marginally disabled, tennis-trim legs would carry her.

Mallory smiled again. 'I'm fine here. As long as I can stretch out my leg,' and he stiffened his left leg so that it pressed firmly and obtrusively against Bunty's knee. It was like a metre-long

124

erection, and it was all Bunty could do not to slap it away like a nurse with a naughty patient. In fact, that's exactly what he was like, a matron character from a *Carry On* film. 'So … you like the hotel? Lounge,' she blurted, correcting herself quickly before Randy the Old Goat could suggest checking it out.

'I love it,' said Mallory, and for a moment his craggy features softened. 'I used to come here a lot with my wife when they did tea dances on a Sunday afternoon.' In the thirties? Bunty thought, trying very hard not to show that she was calculating his age. 'They did them right up to the seventies when that chain took over,' added Mallory, gesturing to the waiter for tea.

'Oh! Oh, and with your wife,' said Bunty. 'Priscilla told me you were widowed early.' She hadn't said 'early last century', but she had said 'early.'

'When she was forty-six,' said Mallory with a sigh. 'Your age. You look very like her.'

'I'm thirty-eight!' squeaked Bunty. Priscilla had done a little more age-massaging, it seemed.

'Oh, I'm sorry. Not such a good judge, eh, Mallory? I find I can't tell the difference between thirty and fifty-five any more. You women keep yourself in such good shape.' Mallory leaned forward and patted Bunty's thigh in what he appeared to think was an avuncular fashion but which definitely involved a little rub of a gnarled thumb across her skin. Goose bumps ran up her leg instantly, bumps of horror rather than libido.

Edging her knee out of the way as subtly as she could, Bunty drained her cup and poured herself another hasty cup of coffee. She needed something to do with her hands, something to stop her slapping dirty old Mallory across the wizened cheek when bits of him started to roam again. Chancing a surreptitious glance in his direction, she found that he was stirring his tea wistfully, and suddenly he looked less like some black-and-white movie Lothario and more like … well, more like a lonely old man. Be kind, Bunty, she told herself.

'Did you fancy a cake as well?' she said. 'They had a lovely bakewell tart on that trolley in the corner.'

His eyes lit up. 'Ah, you know how to cheer old Mallory up. I love a bit of tart.'

'Mallory …'

'Bakewell tart, I mean. Or jam.'

Bunty waved the waiter over, settling into her chair. She had the measure of him now, this elderly gentleman who talked about himself in the third person, perhaps because nobody said his name much any more, and who clearly still longed for a friendly touch, for some physical contact. 'When did your wife die, Mallory?'

His answer was unexpected. 'Ten years ago.' He peered up at Bunty mischievously. 'Yes, she was a lot younger than me. Twenty-one years between us. Kept me young at heart. What about you?'

'Young at heart? Well, yes I like to think so. I'm not actually that old anyway.' I'm roughly half his age, Bunty worked out quickly. 'Oh, you mean, was I widowed? No.' She shook her head. 'My husband's … trading me in.'

At this Mallory's rheumy eyes became even more opaque. 'Bunty, Bunty. How could anyone want for a more lovely companion than yourself? Silly man. You should be cherished. Looked after.'

'I couldn't agree more,' said Bunty with a grin.

'That's how Mallory likes to treat a woman. With dignity. Respect. And a good bit of how's your father.' His eyes twinkled with devilment, and Bunty could suddenly see what an attractive man he must have been, not so very long ago either. Nonetheless, he had just inadvertently introduced her father into the conversation, and she suppressed a shudder.

It was time for a bit of straight talking, and, feeling surprisingly relaxed, Bunty opted for complete honesty. 'You do know, Mallory, that I'm not that woman – the one you want to treat with respect and dignity and … what have you? You're very charming, but you might want to think about someone closer to your age? Us younger women these days, well …' She paused as she came to her conclusion. 'I don't think we're very nice.'

Mallory laughed with a sound of crackling cellophane. 'You look pretty nice to old Mallory!'

'Don't you believe it,' said Bunty, pouring him more tea. 'We're demanding and contrary, and we're never happy. Never content to settle for second best. Always thinking there's something more interesting around the corner. Would you want to work that hard?'

'Good Lord above, no.' Bunty could see that Mallory looked quite appalled at the prospect. 'I just want someone who's happy with … just with me, I suppose. Content with old Mallory and a bit of bakewell tart for elevenses. And whatever they fancy for supper,' he added lasciviously.

Bunty munched on some bakewell tart thoughtfully. It really was very good. 'Do you know what,' she said suddenly. 'I may know the perfect person. How are you with dead cats?'

Mallory didn't skip a beat. 'More of a dog man, I must say, but since I lost dear old Benson I haven't really got the heart for another animal. They fill such a space, you know.'

And Bunty made a quick, potentially rash decision. 'I'm having dinner for a few friends on Saturday. Why don't you come? Not to be with me, but to meet someone I know.'

'Love to, my dear,' said Mallory eagerly.

Bunty scribbled the address on the back of a coaster and handed it to him as she gathered up her coat. 'And one word about where we met and I'll thrash your good leg.'

'Oh, promises, promises,' purred Mallory.

Well, she thought as she headed round to Mary's to offer an invitation. Maybe dinner with Ryan and Petra – and Graham – wouldn't be quite so dull after all.

CHAPTER TWELVE

It was only as she drove home that Bunty realised the full impact of what she had just arranged – a Ray Cooney farce in her own dining room. The cast list would be:

Graham: Paunchy financial advisor with mid-life crisis, having an affair.

Bunty: Put-upon, cuckolded wife, trying to invent a new life for herself.

Ryan: Nasal and nerdy finance man, with the hots for Bunty.

Petra: Nasal and nerdy wife of finance man, no redeeming features, not even hots.

Mary: Bereaved widow and beloved neighbour.

Mallory: Bereaved widower and septuagenarian sex fiend.

Charlotte: Charlotte.

Charlotte? What the hell was she going to do with Charlotte while six supposedly grown people batted double entendres back and forth across the table? And Mallory – why on earth had she invited Mallory? It had seemed like a good idea at the time, but if he couldn't tell the difference between thirty and fifty-five there was a strong chance he wouldn't be able to tell the difference between thirteen and thirty-three. Charlotte would have to stay completely out of the way. And he could easily let slip about the Croesus Club. Perhaps she'd have to gag him. Although he'd probably like that. And Mary! Fancy inflicting Mallory the Mauler on poor, dignified Mary. What in God's name had she been thinking?

She headed straight down the road parallel to her own and knocked at Mary's door. No time like the present for a very back-handed invitation which she almost hoped Mary would refuse. There was no reply, so Bunty wandered down the side path and out into the back garden, following the squeak of the rotary clothesline. 'Mary, I ... oh! Hi, Dan.'

Mary and Dan looked up from the graveside. 'Look,' said Mary, dotting a tear away on yet another laundered handkerchief – pink this time to match Mary's Marks & Spencer polo neck and cardigan, teamed today to contrast prettily with her neat brown trousers. For a lady in her seventies, she dressed very well. Bunty followed her crooked finger to the little mound of earth at their feet. 'Look what Dan did.'

Dan grinned sheepishly, looking suddenly like an overgrown school-kid in his serviceable overalls. 'I told you, Mary, it was nothing. I had the stuff spare and ...' He spread his hands towards Bunty in a manner that meant 'Can you take over?' Sobbing elderly ladies were clearly not in his remit.

Bunty put her head on one side and considered Dan's masterpiece. Flinders' new grave had been sited quite high up behind a small retaining wall, in the flower bed that used to house Colin's collection of potted fuchsias. There was a little mound of earth in a carefully regulated rectangle, with a border of small white rings that looked like lace but turned out, on closer inspection, to be neat slender slices of three inch drainpipe. Mounted on the top was a small grey cross (guttering?) on which someone – Dan, presumably – had painted the cat's name in neat gloss letters. A small pot of purple-tipped fuchsias danced nearby, adding just the right hint of colour. And life.

'All waterproof and not blocking anything,' hissed Dan out of the corner of his mouth. 'The cat's in a 12-inch rain trap.'

Bunty put an arm around the pair of them. 'That's truly beautiful,' she said, giving Mary's shoulder a squeeze. 'Mary, Flinders will never have to be moved again. Dan, you're very, very kind.'

'Colin would have loved it.' Mary sniffled loudly into her hanky.

Oh God. Colin. How could Bunty possibly mention Mallory and dinner when they were standing over the cat Colin had loved in the garden he'd nurtured.

Dan coughed. 'Glad you like it. And, of course, your drains are cleared now.'

'Oh-oo! Daniel.' Mary swatted at him and giggled like … well, Charlotte, actually. Bunty whipped her head between the two of them. Was that a bit of a flirt? A slightly dirty flirt, for that matter?

'Mary!'

'Oh, now, Bunty. Don't look like that. Even us older women enjoy a bit of … you know, dirty drains talk.'

'Colin handy with the old plunger, was he, Mary?' said Dan with a cheeky nudge of the elbow. Mary cackled madly.

'Dan! Mary!' Bunty shook her head at the pair of them. 'I'll have to cover Flinders' ears.'

'Tosh,' said Mary, stuffing her handkerchief up her sleeve. Bunty half-expected to see leather bracelets hidden up there too. 'Flinders could have told you a thing or two, that's for sure.'

This was unbelievable. 'Am I the only one without a sex life?' Bunty blurted. 'Oh God, did I say that out loud?'

Mary and Dan shrugged at each other, sniggering. Clearly she *was* the only one without a sex life. Or a recent one, at any rate. Still, clearly she need have no qualms about setting Mallory on Mary and adding her to her cast list. Damn. Dinner list. 'Mary, when you've quite calmed down,' she said with a grin, 'we're having a dinner party on Saturday, and I wondered if you'd like to come. There's a … friend I'd like to introduce you to.'

Mary's papery face lit up like a harvest moon. 'Dinner? Friends? How lovely! Oh, thank you, Bunty. Can I make something?'

'Oh my word, yes.' Two birds, one stone, thought Bunty. Keep Mary feeling useful, and avoid the need to make all three courses herself. 'Could you bring dessert?'

'I'll make an apple betty.' Mary looked over at the apple tree, ready to start picking there and then, and at the same moment Dan and Bunty remembered what had been festering around the roots. Dead cat and human crap betty didn't have quite the same allure.

'Tell you what I like,' said Dan quickly. 'A nice peach cobbler.'

Mary's eyes lit up. 'Oh yes. So do I. I'll make one just for you, Daniel.'

Oh. So Dan was coming too. 'You are free on Saturday night, Dan,' said Bunty hastily, trying to make it sound like she'd been intending to invite him all along.

'Depends. Have you got a friend for me too?' Dan looked rather pointedly down Bunty's top, and she realised instantly just which friend he meant.

'I'll see if Kat's free,' she said with a sigh. Holy shit! Forget Ray Cooney and polite, air-clappy, titter-titter theatre. This was going to be like an episode of *Survivor*. She'd have to kill them all off one by one just to make sure she was the one who made it to the end. Maybe apply betty wasn't such a bad idea after all.

Charlotte was stoical, in her teenage fashion, about the prospect of an evening with six – no, eight – 'olds' around the place. 'Well, du-uh. I know when I'm not wanted. And I don't want to come to your stupid dinner party. Like, how boring would that be? I'll just stay in my bedroom. Okayyyy?'

She bared the whites of her eyes at Bunty, for some inexplicable reason, before traipsing disconsolately from the room. Bunty thought about it for a moment, hand on hip, caught in the middle of a movement. Caught in the middle, again.

All she'd said was, 'Dad and I have got some work people round to dinner on Saturday. You could go to the movies with a friend – my treat.' Somehow between her lips and Charlotte's ears that had apparently turned into 'Get out of our way, we don't want you around while we're doing grown up things' and that had put Charlotte on the defensive. Of course, that was more or less what she'd meant, but somehow everything Bunty said to

Charlotte these days was seen as something combative. Sometimes she even thought twice about opening her mouth at all, knowing that whatever she said would come out the wrong way, or be taken the wrong way, or most certainly would be answered the wrong way. Kids. Who'd have 'em. Bunty thought fleetingly of Ben, of the touching little vista she'd drawn in her mind's eye of Ben's little darlings fitting somehow into their new conjoined life. She batted the thought away defiantly. 'Don't need it. Okayyyyy,' she said, mimicking Charlotte's rolling eyeballs.

'I'm sorry?' During her reverie, Graham had entered the lounge dressed fetchingly in his socks and boxers, shirt and tie.

'Nothing,' she said quickly. 'Argument with Charlotte.'

Graham just nodded. There were plenty of those to go round. He didn't need any details. 'Should I wear a tie for dinner?'

Just as she was about to launch into a 'why would you and who cares anyway' sort of speech, Bunty took a look at his shirt. It was new. White. Fitted. The tie was also new and a rather fetching purple shade. And back to that shirt. It was definitely fitted. 'That's new,' she said accusingly. 'It's … nice,' she added, even more accusingly.

Was he actually blushing? Bunty watched, amazed, as Graham slid his hands down over the shirt. 'I've lost a bit of weight,' he said, almost apologetically. 'My old work shirts were getting a bit big.'

Yeah, and a bit old, and a bit crusty around the armpits, and a bit not-right-for-Kylie, she wanted to say. But she stopped herself. For tonight, at least, he seemed to be making an effort.

There was no harm in her doing the same. 'No tie,' she said eventually. 'And leave the shirt out, over your jeans.'

It was how Ben had worn his shirt, and it had looked amazing. Even Graham managed to look reasonable dressed that way; slightly cute even, with his little Shrek ears, pink and smelling of Lifebuoy, bobbing above his open collar.

In the end, Bunty settled for a similar look herself, with tight jeans, a fitted linen shirt that showed just a hint of lacy bra, and strappy shoes. She didn't want to make too much effort, as there was actually nobody there she wanted to impress – and she'd definitely rather not inflame Ryan if at all possible, or Mallory for that matter – but she was still quite pleased with the result. At least she didn't look like a woman about to be dumped by her present husband and already dumped by her future one. On impulse, she grabbed a tiny diamante hairpin from Charlotte's room and shoved it among her short dark curls, where it glinted like a snowflake.

'That's mine,' whined Charlotte, spotting it even from the bottom of the stairs. She had a nose for anything taken from her small stock of fripperies, which was strangely at odds with her willingness to filch anything from shoes to vintage winter coats from her mother's wardrobe.

'You look nice, Mum. Nice shoes, Mum,' said Bunty plaintively as she came down towards her.

'Yeah, well, you would look nice; that's *my* hair clip.'

Bunty gave up. 'Have you had your tea?'

'Some rubbish out of the freezer. Enjoy your lovely dinner,' said Charlotte. 'I'll just be in my room. On my own. Starving.'

'You're welcome to have some, but it's lamb,' said Bunty. 'I could bring it up on a plate.'

Charlotte held up a hand at the top of the stairs. The teenage stop sign. Go no further. At least she didn't tell Bunty to 'talk to' it. 'I'm fine. You just enjoy yourself. And don't drink too much. And if anyone's smoking send them outside because I don't want that poison in my lungs. Ever. Okay?'

Once again the tables had turned. Bunty half-waited for Charlotte to tell her to be in at a reasonable hour, young lady. She was distracted by the doorbell.

Mary and Dan were standing side by side on the doorstep bearing a pie dish and a bottle of wine respectively, for all the world as though they'd stepped out of a clock and were just about to set off in different directions along the front path. 'Sorry if we're a bit early,' said Dan quietly. Bunty could see instantly that he'd had trouble with Mary.

'It's seven, isn't it, Bunty? That's what time you said.'

Bunty checked her watch – 7.01. 'It is indeed, Mary, come on in.'

Mary stepped inside and held out her arms. 'Cobbler. I don't know what the matter is with Dan. He wanted to be 'fashionably late' whatever that means. I told him, seven o'clock means seven o'clock. And I normally have my tea at five thirty so I'm more than ready by now. Everyone must be famished by seven.'

'I quite agree, ma'am,' said a mellifluous, Donald Sinden type voice from behind them. Mallory had made quite an effort with his appearance, and was looking quite the gentleman in a three-piece suit complete with fob watch, which he was studying on the door step. 'Seven oh two. I do hope I'm not late, Bunty dearest.'

Fortunately Graham had heard the commotion and stepped into corporate mode. 'Mary, hello, come on in. I've got a nice sherry waiting for you. And this is … Mallory, hello. Sherry for you too? Straight through to the lounge. And you must be Dan.' He clapped Dan's hand heartily – Bunty almost expected a matey hug. But then they'd gone, discussing which beer they were going to have and how Chelsea was going to do in the league. It was a Graham she used to hate, taking charge, moving things along, being orderly and work-orientated. For now, however, it was a bit of a relief, and she left him in charge of cloakroom duties as Ryan, Petra and Kat arrived all at once, while she sought refuge in the kitchen.

Kat shimmied in with a bottle and poured out a large glass for Bunty. 'Graham neglecting the chef again? I must say, he's almost looking a bit tasty tonight.'

'Dan?'

'No, Graham.'

'What!'

Kat shrugged. 'Well, for Graham, I mean. Must suit him, having this affair.'

'Talking of which,' said Bunty, changing the subject as quickly as possible, 'I think Dan has his eye on you. Bits of you at any rate.'

'Oooh. Nice.' Kat gave a little satisfied smile. 'Could be a good night then.'

Bunty slammed down the hot dish of coquilles saint-jacques. 'Kat! God, what is wrong with everyone? It's like everyone's in season! Even bloody Mary.'

'Oh, that sounds good,' said Dan from the edge of the dining area.

Bunty sighed. 'What does?'

'Bloody mary. Have you got some on the go?'

'I'll make some,' said Kat eagerly, and she scurried behind Bunty for the jug. 'I'm not going to do anything,' she whispered to Bunty. 'It's just a bit of a flirt. Relax!'

Bunty blinked rapidly, pretending to wipe the steam from her eyes. Relax. Yes. That was all she had to do. Pretend she hadn't invented the dinner party from hell, and that her husband wasn't dallying with a Day-glo accessoried bimbette with a bottom, and that she wasn't the only one here without at least one love interest in the offing. Relax. Flirt. She used to be the expert at it. That was her sport. Forget archery or tennis – a night of naughty asides and fluttering of the eyelashes used to be how she got through the evening, reminded herself she was attractive, wanted – alive, somehow. And of course it was never meant to go anywhere, because there was always Graham; but now there wasn't, not for long anyway, and flirting could actually lead to something. But with who? She knew who, of course. But he wasn't there.

So she tried to relax, and somehow, despite all her rather depressing thoughts and her constant fear that someone was going to drop a *faux pas* onto the table and let slip all about her Croesus activities, the evening was, well, fun, she supposed.

Mallory was a marvellous raconteur and held them all, Mary especially, completely spellbound with his tales of the area during the Blitz, and Beatlemania, and the three-day week. Ryan and Petra were overwhelmingly grey; in fact, Ryan only flushed when Kat asked, half-innocently, 'So, Ryan, are you Graham's squash partner?'

'Squash?' Petra laughed. 'Ryan has bad knees. You can't play squash, can you, darling? He can't play squash,' she confirmed for the rest of them.

'Oh.' Kat feigned confusion, pouting so prettily that Dan leaned in and practically fell down her cleavage. 'Oh, sorry, only, Graham, I thought that Bunty had said you'd taken up squash with Ryan. Or was it football with Ryan? You two will have to be careful, anyway. People will talk.'

'What about?' said Graham, a tad more sharply than was necessary. Or usual.

'They'll be saying, Is that Graham having an affair,' and Kat peered provocatively around the table à la Miss Marple, 'with Ryan?'

Peels of raucous laughter echoed around the room, largely from Kat, laughing at her own joke, from Mallory, who clearly thought the idea of homosexuality was preposterous, and Ryan, whose laugh whistled through his adenoids like a zephyr up the Grand Canyon. He evidently had asthma, too, as well as terminal blandness, Bunty realised. He'd never played squash in his life. Yet he was somehow complicit with Graham. That much was clear from the exchange of glances and the look of relief that swept over Graham's rosy face when Kat inadvertently removed the focus from what they were actually up to.

'It's only because they're –' said Petra suddenly, not seeing the funny side of it, but then there was a furtive shuffling under the table. She coloured and corrected herself. 'Friends,' she said firmly. 'Only because they're friends. They're not gay. You're not gay, are you, Ryan? He's not gay,' she finished for him before he had time to deny the charges.

There was a long awkward pause, and then Dan said quietly, 'Oh, that's a shame. Cos I am.' And he fluttered his ridiculously black eyelashes at Ryan and then Mallory.

'You're gay?' shrieked Kat.

'No!' Dan laughed uproariously, and everyone else joined in. Bunty smiled at him thankfully. For all his shovel-handed, manly, smelly-job front, 'Dan, Dan the Drainage Man' had a certain social charm that made all those around him feel, well, happy. She'd never met a man so comfortable in his own skin. Graham, meanwhile, was currently so uncomfortable in his that he was about to burst out of it like an overcooked sausage.

'Relax,' she said, filling his glass with a rather good Lafite he'd dragged out of the back of a cupboard. He'd been saving it for Kylie, no doubt.

He gave her a long, searching look; a look that she couldn't interpret properly, but which seemed to be checking out whether she'd worked out what was going on. She stared back at him levelly, inscrutable, and then finally he chinked his glass against hers and drained the contents into his mouth. That look she understood, after so many years of translating his every grunt.

'We might be having a crisis,' it said, 'but we've just agreed we're not going to have it tonight.'

And they didn't. Lamb, mangetout and new potatoes segued neatly into peach cobbler and crème fraîche, then port, more wine, chocolates provided by Kat, and then goodnights, and swapping of numbers, and a gentlemanly kiss of Mary's hand from Mallory. It was all going so smoothly that Graham even dared to drop a vaguely proprietorial hand onto her shoulder as they waved Kat off in a cab, laughing as Dan made a very obvious grab for her breasts and then shouted, 'Couldn't resist, sorry. I've never seen boobs that were bigger than my hands before.'

'They're spoken for,' squealed Kat, then she blew everyone a kiss and disappeared into the night.

Graham shook his head as he closed the door. 'She's mad,' he said, though without the usual slight chilly edge of disapproval that he normally reserved for Kat. 'And that was fun.'

'It was. It really was,' said Bunty. She could hardly believe it herself. Other than the odd little social slip it had been really quite an evening, pleasant and flowing and more of a giggle than she'd had in ages, since she and Kat and Cally had last been out together. 'Quite like the old days.'

For a moment she and Graham looked at each other, both remembering their early dinner parties; not quite on a packing case because Graham had already collected some sensible furniture from his grandmother, but nonetheless on mismatched chairs and one ordinary fork in the fondue pot, and too much

141

cheap wine and bad games of Pictionary … and as she smiled at the memory she came to with a start. Graham was running a finger along her lip.

It was another thing she remembered very well.

'You look about twenty-two,' said Graham, and he leaned in to kiss her.

And even though she wasn't completely against the idea; even though Graham looked younger himself than he had in … well, forever, and even though this same evening in the past would definitely have led to sex, possibly even with a degree of enthusiasm, the worm in her mind wouldn't stop turning. 'Is that how old you like them these days? Twenty-two?'

Graham stopped a millimetre away from her mouth. 'What are you on about?' he said softly.

'You know. Your squash partners. Twenty-two? Or, God, it's not younger is it?'

'What …' Graham looked genuinely bewildered, then something occurred to him. 'This isn't about that computer stuff, is it? Because I've already told you that wasn't me. Or … Jesus, you don't think Ryan and I are really … you couldn't think that!'

Bunty shrugged, feeling unaccountably hurt all of a sudden. He couldn't even do the decent thing and confess. 'I don't know what I think.'

'Well, whatever it is,' said Graham, breathing hard, no longer from passion, 'it isn't good, is it? We … we should talk.'

The phone vibrated in her jeans pocket, but as she went to grab it, Graham got hold of her hand, stopping her. 'Bun, not now, this is important.'

There was a phone number. A number starting with 0064.

New Zealand.

Ben.

'So's this,' said Bunty. She walked down the hall and pressed the button.

When she turned round, Graham was already walking up the stairs to bed.

CHAPTER THIRTEEN

Pearl: Today we're very pleased to have with us this year's Super Mummy, Bunty McKenna. Bunty, welcome.

Bunty (*inclining head graciously*): Pleasure, Pearl.

Finn: Ooops! Pleasure Pearl. Sounds like something a bit naughty.

Pearl (*giggles*): Finn. Now, we're actually here to talk about something very serious, that might affect a lot of parents out there. Bunty, tell us more. What did you find in the bedroom that night?

Finn (*barely suppressing a snort*). Don't tell me – a pleasure pearl. Ha!

He leans sideways out of camera shot, giggling even harder, and Pearl starts to shudder with restrained laughter.

Bunty: (*stern, Super-Mummyish*): Actually, it was in my daughter's bedroom, and it's something I hope all parents will take notice of. You see, while my husband and I were having a dinner party, my daughter was upstairs emailing her friend in New Zealand. Her friend recommended a certain children's book (*she holds up the offending best-seller*), and my daughter Charlotte keyed in the name.

Pearl: Only she didn't get a website featuring that character, did she?

Bunty: No. She keyed in one of the letters incorrectly, and what came up was a horrendous site featuring … um … Russian ladies of ill repute and their collection of, well, sex toys, I suppose you'd have to call them.

Finn: Like … like Pleasure Pearls! Oh. Stop, please!

He sinks to his knees before the sofa, crippled with mirth, and Pearl begins to join in.

Bunty: It's not funny. It's not funny. This is serious. It's not funny.

'It's not funny. It's not …'

'Funny. You said,' muttered Graham, banging the pillow more firmly around his ears.

Bunty opened her eyes. Graham's smooth back appeared to stare at her reproachfully, and she studied it for a moment as she pulled her thoughts together. Had he waxed? She couldn't honestly remember whether his back used to be this hairless or not. That wasn't funny either – not at all amusing to be unable to recall whether your husband had gone from barely washing to now having back, sack and crack done. (She'd seen the procedure on a magazine show, or was it one of those Japanese torture things?)

But definitely not funny was the realisation that your children searching for things on the internet could put in an innocent name and up would pop Madame Vanya with her array of helpful products.

It hadn't been Ben on the phone at all. It had been Cally.

'Bunty,' she said, 'what has Charlotte been doing?'

Bunty bridled, but only for a moment. She didn't really like the fact that Cally would instantly assume that Charlotte had been up to no good, but she did have some basis for it, since Charlotte had been the cause of quite a lot of trouble in the past. 'What do you mean? She's just been upstairs while we've been having a dinner party.'

Cally paused, and Bunty could tell that under any other circumstances she would have been dying to hear what that was all about, but then she said, 'Well, it's 10.30 in the morning here, and Paige has just come out of her bedroom to ask me what a dildo is. Yes, you heard right. A dildo.'

'You shouldn't leave your stuff lying around then, should you? You and Pete and your kinky love-life.'

'Bunty, even if I had one of those, *and* I left it lying around, I wouldn't stick a big label on it saying what it's called, would I?'

'It could be in its box,' Bunty suggested.

'Are you drunk or something? Oh, I suppose you might be. Okay. Bunty McKenna, go upstairs now and see what your daughter is up to on the computer, because she and Paige have been emailing for the last hour and that's how it happened.'

'Oh shit,' said Bunty, finally realising that Cally was serious.

Still clutching the phone, Bunty pelted up the stairs, barely wobbling in her high heels, and flung open Charlotte's door. Charlotte nearly jumped out of her skin but then turned round with kohl-rimmed eyes so horrified that Bunty knew whatever she'd done had been a mistake. Or it might not have started out as a mistake, but it had gone too far.

A hideous image of Madame Vanya, boobs and bottom strapped down with a few thongs of leather and very little else,

146

with something like a telegraph cucumber in her hand, winked from the laptop screen. Graham's laptop. Bunty's first thought, as she reached out and shut it down as quickly as was humanly possible after the best part of a bottle of heavy red, was that this was another part of Graham's slummy little secret. But then Charlotte, bottom lip wobbling, suddenly said, 'Mum, I'm sorry, I didn't do it on purpose, and I was only trying to look up this book that Paige likes, 'Vanta Paradise' or something and all these horrible pictures came up and … what *are* all those things?'

'You didn't go any further into the site?' said Bunty, hardly daring to imagine what Charlotte, still so innocent despite all her bravado, might have seen.

'Ugh, no. It's *gross*!' Charlotte shuddered dramatically and shoved the laptop back into its bag. 'I am never going on the computer again.'

'Bunty! Bunty!' called a tinny voice. Bunty looked around, convinced for one surreal moment that Madame Vanya was calling to her from the laptop, then remembered her mobile phone.

'Bun, I heard all that. I'm sure it was just a mistake,' said Cally.

'I think so.' Bunty sat down hard on the bed, her heart suddenly thumping against her rib cage. 'Oh God, how awful. She's banned from computers from now on.'

'Paige too,' said Cally.

'But how will they keep in touch?'

'They can talk on the phone, or write letters to each other. Then we can vet them like they're prisoners. Which, of course, they are.' Cally sounded woolly for a moment, then tuned back in on the other end of the phone. 'Look, sorry, I'd better go. David's waking up and Pete's not back from refereeing yet to give him his bottle.'

'You mean you've got to feed your own child?'

'Outrageous, isn't it? Bye, Bun-hun.'

Bunty's whole body drooped as the phone went dead. God, she missed Cally. Charlotte missed Paige too. What were they doing a world away from each other? Well, invoking global witchery in the form of Madame Vanya, it appeared.

'Mum,' said a small voice next to her. Charlotte's hand crept into hers. 'Would you read to me? I want to get those sicko pictures out of my head.' She made outrageous vomiting noises just to demonstrate how sick they'd been.

Bunty almost cried. Her little girl was back. Only for a moment, perhaps, and down to very dubious causes, but she was going to cherish it. Together they squashed onto Charlotte's single bed and read *Little Women*, which was about as wholesome a book as Bunty could lay hands on, and only later, long after Marmee had administered soup to the needy of the district and Charlotte had fallen asleep on her shoulder, depositing a goodly amount of lumpy mascara onto her linen shirt, did Bunty ease herself out of the bed and the room, and slide in next to Graham, still fully dressed apart from her shoes. After the sight of Madame Vanya there was a strong possibility she would never take her clothes off again.

Now she had woken up after her slightly twisted dream about Pearl and Finn – not that it was their fault in any way, but she was starting to see them in rather a different light now – she felt oddly calm. Resolved. Today was a new day. She would attempt to talk to Graham about his 'situation'. She would forget about the Croesus Club and all that it entailed. And she would monitor every waking second of Charlotte's day, with much the same assiduous attention that she had devoted to stalking Ben. Oh. Who? Yeah, nobody.

Charlotte needed them. That much was evident. And if Graham was too wrapped up in Kylie Smiley Pert Bum to care then she, Bunty McKenna, Super Mummy, would step into the breach.

Of course, she reminded herself as she stared at the ceiling thinking about Charlotte's white and horrified face, it was a mistake to assume that their daughter hadn't noticed the atmosphere about the place. It would have been very evident to her that her father was out more often (which she may have been glad about, having professed to hate him so much a couple of years ago that she'd even tried to find a new dad for herself). Bunty had also recognised the wide-eyed curiosity now accompanying the goodbyes whenever she, too, was heading out the door, taking up a new 'sport', meeting Kat yet again for a little drink, or hosting bizarre dinner parties with people she barely knew and who'd not long before been up to their armpits in sewage.

Yes, Charlotte was pretty savvy, despite her apparent detachment from their world. Or the world in general. And they hadn't given this a whole lot of consideration. Bunty had merely assumed that Charlotte would live with her, and that Graham would go on to spawn little Kylie look-alikes with wife number two and would sideline Charlotte over the years. She'd be relegated. On the bench. Suddenly Bunty was filled with a fury so intense at what Graham was about to do their only child that she had to tussle with a very strong temptation to clamp the ear-covering pillow around his face, and squeeze. They had to talk. She was just wondering how to open the conversation ('So, Graham, when you leave me ...') when Graham lifted himself up on one elbow, stared wildly at the clock over her shoulder, then screamed 'Bollocks!' straight down into her ear.

How had he known what she was going to say? 'There's no bloody need for that. You just perforated my eardrum. And it's not bollocks, it's very important ...'

'Sorry, sorry,' muttered Graham, flinging back the duvet and flying out of bed. He took a backwards glance at her. 'Fully clothed? So that's what it's come to now, has it? I wasn't that desperate for sex, you know.' He hauled some tracksuit bottoms out of a drawer and staggered around the bedroom getting into them in too much of a hurry.

'I bet you weren't,' said Bunty sourly. Already getting plenty, no doubt. 'And that's typical, that is. It was nothing to do with you. Nothing. You didn't see Madame Vanya wrapped in duct tape. Or maybe you did! It was on your laptop, for Chrissakes!'

150

'Not that again!' roared Graham, bouncing into his trainers. 'There's nothing dodgy on my fucking laptop!'

'Well, tell that to your daughter, and to … to Social Services when they come round,' screamed Bunty, so infuriated that she grabbed his abandoned pillow and thwacked him with it, 'and to whoever you're dashing off to now, while she …' (thwack) 'cuts off …' (thwack to the left, parry to the right) 'your scrotum!'

Graham caught hold of the other end of the pillow and stared at her as she panted, her logic muddled, her emotions coursing. It was the first, the only time that either of them had ever resorted to violence, other than the odd tiny foray into Madame Vanya territory. 'You've gone mad,' he said eventually, thrusting the pillow to one side. 'Completely fucking barking. Now, let's just calm down, eh? I have to go to play squash,' he said, pulling a tee shirt over his almost defined shoulders. And no, it's not with Ryan. And no, it's not with some nutty woman who is going to neuter me. I suggest you have a cup of tea, take a few deep breaths, and get a sense of perspective.'

'Don't tell me to get a perspective, you patronising arsehole.' And for some reason, after shrieking the last word at Graham, she burst into loud sobs. 'You get one! You!'

Charlotte appeared at the door. 'You two okay?' she said quietly. She looked like she might be thinking about crying. 'You woke me up.'

'Sorry, love,' said Graham. 'Think we might have had a bad glass of wine last night or something. I'm going out to, um, you know, play squash. Hey,' he said, ruffling Charlotte's hair, 'why don't you come with me?'

She looked up at him under her fringe. 'I don't have to, like, play, do I?'

'Nah. Bring a book or something. I'll buy you a hot chocolate afterwards.'

'Okay.'

Charlotte wandered off behind Graham to get dressed, trying to look nonchalant but evidently very pleased at getting some 'dad' time. Bunty sank her head onto her knees. 'Great start,' she moaned. So that was how it was to be – battling for Charlotte's attention, bribing her with bigger and bigger incentives to spend time with him. It was a far cry from the days when Charlotte never wanted to leave her side. But then, there had been days – and how she'd detested them – when Graham never wanted to leave her side either. And where were they going? Was he introducing Charlotte to the other woman? Had Charlotte already met her? God! It could be someone they already knew, someone Charlotte wouldn't consider odd to be meeting for a hot chocolate on a Sunday morning. Who could that be? Petra? A neighbour? Kat?

With all this tumbling through her head Bunty stumbled out of bed, hearing the door slam and her phone ring on the dressing table at the exact same moment. The screen showed 0064 … A New Zealand number again. It made sense – roughly ten hours later; it would be late evening in New Zealand, and Cally would know she'd be up by now.

'Okay, okay, I can promise you that we've just been asleep,' she said in as perky a tone as she could muster. 'Definitely no more bondage or vibrators since we spoke.'

There was a long pause, during which Bunty worried for a second that Cally might have her on loudspeaker so that Paige, Pete, possibly even the baby would be looking at each other in shocked bewilderment. Then a deep voice said, 'You know, I have absolutely no idea how to respond to that.'

'Oh God. Ben.' Finally. 'I thought you were someone else.' She knew as she said it that it was ambiguous, that he might think there had actually been some bondage going on with another person, another man . But sod it, she thought. Let him. She'd every right to get it on – or off – with someone else since he'd disappeared out of her life. No opportunity, but every right.

Ben clearly took it the wrong way, almost as she'd intended. 'Right. Well, I deserve that, I guess.'

'You do a bit.'

Ben laughed. 'I know. I owe you a massive apology. That day we were meant to meet I found out that my ex was introducing my kids to, you know, the new bloke. It sort of screwed with my head a bit.'

'Oh, Ben.' So that was it. It was perfectly reasonable. He'd been upset and gone to ground. And wasn't she going through the very same thing, right at that very moment? 'That's awful. I totally understand. So you're back in New Zealand now?'

'No,' said Ben, sounding puzzled. 'Oh, the phone number. That's my old phone. I bought a new one to use here but I'm afraid I got a bit mad when my ex rang to tell me the lovely news, and I …' He laughed softly, as if he could hardly believe it himself. 'Well, to be honest I threw the phone on the ground and jumped up and down on it. I really, really lost it.'

'Aw,' said Bunty, trying to sound sympathetic but also going slightly mushy inside at how cute he sounded saying, 'Rurly, rurly lost ut.' He wasn't in New Zealand. He was still around. And he was calling her! Suddenly the morning looked so much brighter.

Easy does it, though, Bunty, she thought. 'So have you got your head back together then?'

'I think so.'

'Well, I'm glad. And I do understand, you know, Ben. You could have just told me.'

Ben groaned. 'I know. I just wasn't thinking straight. But I am now, and I was just wondering if your ex has your daughter today. I mean, are you free now? I shouldn't even ask.'

'No! I mean, yes. Yes, he does have Charlotte right now, so I suppose … I suppose I'm free.' She moved the phone closer to her mouth so he wouldn't hear the pulse throbbing in her throat.

'It's a beautiful day. Maybe you could find that picnic blanket again.'

Bunty restrained the squeal that was about to erupt from her. 'Fine,' she said lightly. 'I'll bring coffee and some sandwiches – cold lamb all right?'

'You're asking a Kiwi if lamb's all right?' Ben laughed. 'I practically am one.'

Well, I'll eat you then, thought Bunty, but she just said, 'See you in twenty minutes, and then I have to be home by twelve.'

'Or you turn into a pumpkin?'

'Midday, not midnight. And never you mind what I turn into.'

There was a long pause, during which Bunty knew that Ben was imagining the bondage, the vibrators, and goodness knew what else. 'Okay. Twenty minutes,' said Ben breathily.

Bunty grinned, squeezed herself, and grinned again as she sprinted down the stairs to the dinner party remains. Very cool, Bunty. Breezy, she told herself. It was back! Her flirt gland had re-engaged. And the recipient was fully engaged too, she guessed. Grabbing the plaid blanket and the picnic, she whisked out to the car.

CHAPTER FOURTEEN

If Bunty had rolled together every romantic film, every 'will-they-won't-they' kiss ever seen on a soap, every single perfect moment of breathy-bosomed costume drama she had ever seen in her life, the sum, to her mind, would still not have matched the pinnacle of exquisite romance that was her reunion kiss with Ben. It was almost exactly as she'd pictured it on the internal movie viewer of her brain as she'd driven at break-neck speed to the hotel at which she'd met Mallory:

1: She rounded the grand facade of the hotel and headed out towards the copse of trees. Ben was standing under one, looking the wrong way. Fantastic. She could check out what he was wearing (long board-shorts, navy polo shirt, flip flops) and admire the ratio of his enormous shoulders to his hand-span waist, take in the still-damp, curly dark hair resting on his collar, and compose herself, all without him knowing.

2. Smiling, she smoothed down her plain white tee-shirt – thrown on in haste with the same jeans she'd worn all night, and the same underwear did he but know it; not that he would have any cause to know it (the trick, she realised, was to leave them *wanting*) – and called out his name.

3. He turned, smiling, watching her face for signs of annoyance then smiling more broadly as he saw there was none. Then he picked her up, straight off her feet, with his nose in the soft space behind her ear, breathing her in, murmuring, 'Thank you! Thank you for not being mad.'

4. As Bunty laughed and kicked a little to be put down, he set her back expertly on her slender, 'not-really-suitable-for-picnics' heels, then gave her a quick kiss on the lips.

5. She kissed him back.

6. He kissed her back.

7. She kissed him back more.

8. He kissed her back again, and then suddenly they were enmeshed in a full-on, breathless grope under the tree, and then against the tree, and then almost behind the tree until a passing gardener screamed 'Hey, get a room!' and they separated, giggling, covering their mouths and their cheeks with mock shame and agreeing, wordlessly, like age-old lovers, to retreat to the blanket and act with some propriety.

It was perfect. Beyond perfect. It was television perfect. (Though Bunty did notice, somewhat to her annoyance, that it later lost something in translation. Kat merely raised her eyebrows, nodded knowingly, and said, 'It's been a looooong time for *that* soldier.'

'What's that supposed to mean?' said Bunty crossly. 'You know,' replied Kat, making lewd rocking motions in her chair. 'He's not *done it* in a while.'

'Well, neither have you, and you don't kiss anyone like that, I bet.' Bunty stopped for a minute. 'You haven't, have you? With Dan?' At which Kat had laughed.

'I told you! I wouldn't do that to Simon.' And somehow the conversation had turned to her long distance relationship, and the agony and ecstasy of Bunty's illicit romance had been side-tracked.)

'Got a bit carried away there,' said Ben. He bit his lip in his embarrassment and inadvertently made Bunty's thighs tingle.

'It's really nice to see you.' Bunty busied herself with the picnic blanket and handed Ben a lamb sarnie before he could make another move. Keep him wanting.

Keeping him talking was the other technique she tried to concentrate on. That was on the advice of Kat, who now considered herself something of an expert having held down a relationship with someone on the other side of the world for over a year. In 'Men According to Kat', the one thing men liked to do almost as much as sex was to talk about themselves. 'That can't be right,' said Bunty, although she did have a vague recollection that Adam had seemed most animated when the discussion was about him. 'Graham doesn't want to talk about anything, hardly ever.'

'But that's not a man,' argued Kat. 'That's Graham.'

Ben bucked the short trend in her life at least a little. While he was very happy to talk about his kids – Jarred who was nearly five and Shanti who was two – and about the yacht, he was very careful to ask questions of Bunty, like 'So what do you do with your time now Charlotte's so grown up?' and 'How far did you get in your fencing?' Mostly Bunty tried to change the subject back to him, because it was more important to make Ben feel relaxed than to think about such matters and lie. Wasn't it?

Once more they snogged like teenagers at a drive-in, and Ben rang next morning to see if he would be allowed to send flowers. 'I know it's not very spontaneous and romantic, but I have to ask you for your address if I'm to send them.'

'Meet me with them!' suggested Bunty, so they met for a quick lunch in a pub garden in a nearby village, and Ben arrived with a bunch of gerbera.

Graham looked askance at the vase as he threw down his bag that night. He was late. Again. 'Where did you get those from?'

'I treated myself,' said Bunty, so aglow with delight that she beamed, even at her husband.

Graham sighed. 'Are they in the budget?'

He did actually work out a household budget at the beginning of each year, and if Bunty had to decide she would probably have to put the flowers under the heading of 'miscellaneous treats and outings' for which she was allowed 100 pounds a month. But this time she had ammo. 'Don't think so, but then I figured, What's going to cost more – cut sperm tubes, or cut flowers? I didn't think a tenner would blow the budget too much.'

'You're still mad about that?'

'I'm still mad, Graham,' she said, picking up his bag pointedly, 'about everything.'

And suddenly she meant it. She wasn't just mad about the vasectomy. She wasn't even mad that he was seeing someone else behind her back. It was bigger than that now, she realised as she kicked his bag into the utility room. Now she was angry that she'd married him in the first place, that she'd given up her chance of an interesting life to be with someone who budgeted for bunches of flowers, and who wouldn't in a million years dream of shoving her up against a tree and kissing the life out of her with a passion that made her feel constantly thirsty. Passion. That was what she was mad about. The lack of passion. She turned the tap on to fill the vase with such ferocity that water sprayed all over them both on either side of the sink.

Quite unexpectedly, Graham grabbed her hand across the breakfast bar. 'Don't be … Don't. It's all going to be over soon, and then you'll see that it's all for the best.'

'What is?' she yelled, then catching Charlotte's eye from where she was lying across her homework at the dining room table, she reeled herself in. 'What is?' she hissed.

'My plan.' Graham blinked at her, as if she should have known all along what his strange male, budgeting brain was working out. 'The plan.'

'Like the plan that we wouldn't have any more children? The plan to take up … extra-curricular activities? Well, just as soon as you decide what my part in this plan is, Graham, you let me know.'

'Mum, can you help me with this maths?' bleated Charlotte.

Bunty wiped her hands on the tea towel and threw it over her shoulder to land on top of Graham's bag. 'Your dad will help you,' she said, staring him down, daring him to say otherwise. 'I'm going out.'

'Now? Who with?' Graham peered round at the oven, which was ominously empty.

'With … me.'

Grabbing her coat and bag, she rushed out to the car. It was 6.30 p.m. Too early to meet Kat, too short notice to call Ben (plus she'd noticed he was no longer using his New Zealand mobile and now had another local phone, for which she couldn't get the number.) But actually, it suddenly occurred to her that

160

she'd just said who she wanted to go out with. Herself. Her beautifully painted ecru walls had closed in on her, and she needed some quiet.

On a whim, Bunty headed out of the city and shot up an A-road to the next market town. The cinema was housed in a converted church – just two screens, often showing independents rather than blockbusters, and sometimes, if she was lucky, something old and black and white. On this particular night she struck gold: a big screen version of *Some Like It Hot*. It was so far from her world that she felt suddenly revived, and the sheer pleasure of buying a ticket for one, and sweets for one so she could dunk her Maltesers in her glass of chardonnay, and getting a seat for one wherever she liked, was a surprise to her. She sank into the seat with an audible sigh. This was better. Here was relief. Peace, in the racket of a machine-gun massacre in downtown twenties Chicago.

Before she could slide down into her seat completely and drop a chocolate into her plastic wine glass, there was a tap on her shoulder, and someone whispered her name.

Oh God, was her first thought. Graham's followed me. Or Jason? She turned around with some trepidation to find Dan's smiling face a few inches from her own. 'I thought that was you. All right?'

'I'm fine. One of my favourite films,' she whispered back.

Dan pointed back along the row. 'My mum's too. We're just over there if you want to join us.'

'You brought your mum to see her favourite film? Dan, you have got to be gay.'

161

'No. Just nice,' said Dan with a smile. 'We do exist, you know.'

Bunty nodded, and then indicated that she wanted to stay put. Giving her a thumbs up, Dan shuffled back to his mum's side, where Bunty could hear the two of them chuckling together like a pair of geese, Dan's booming honk to his mum's gentle titter.

It was only nine o'clock when the film finished. Bunty waved to Dan and his mum, then got into her car and drove halfway around the M25. Then she filled up with petrol and drove back along the other half. Driving. That was one of the things she could have said on her resumé. Fencing and driving, particularly at this time of night when she could get her foot down, let her imagination wander and cover ground for no other reason than it was there to do. She walked into the house at midnight, about as calm as she had felt in weeks. Charlotte was asleep on the sofa, with Graham next to her in the armchair, and the television repeating the latest box office news.

Graham opened one eye. 'I can't pick her up any more,' he said sadly, and Bunty suddenly understood why Charlotte was still there. He'd let her fall asleep as they used to on Bunty's rare nights off and out of the house, when he would carry her upstairs at bedtime. Now she was so grown up that she probably had more chance of carrying Graham upstairs, possibly even the two of them together, Dad under one arm, and Mum under the other. It was the first time he'd realised their little girl was really not so little any longer.

Despite that, there was such an uncommon air of peace in the room that Bunty couldn't bear to disturb anyone. She gathered

162

the duvets from upstairs, snuggled down next to Charlotte, and went to sleep to the sound of Graham's snoring.

Charlotte, of course, found it all a huge adventure when she woke up in the morning.

'Did Grandma and Grandad come?' she said with a yawn. That was usually when they – or at least, Charlotte – were turfed out of bed. And they all laughed, even Charlotte, at the truth of the matter whereby Graham couldn't carry her despite his new-found biceps, before she suddenly said, horrified, 'You don't mean I'm, like, *fat*, do you?' and they all laughed again, because she was actually skeletal.

Later that day, Ben asked to meet her for coffee, and she related the tale to him, as he'd lovingly told her tales of his kids, only it got rather broken up with her having to leave Graham out of the picture, and making it sound for a moment as though the babysitter had spent the night in the armchair. Rather like telling Kat about the kiss with Ben, the point of it became somewhat lost and she noticed his eyes glazing over just a fraction. Bunty kicked herself – keep him talking about himself. Mental mantra. Keep him talking.

'Well, this is four days on the trot I've seen you now,' she teased. 'Haven't you got a job to go to? Oh, of course. You're on your yacht.'

Ben shrugged and nodded modestly at the same time. Cally had told Bunty about the Kiwi art of self-deprecation – Ben had definitely managed it.

'So how … is this a rude question? How did you actually make your money? You haven't mentioned your job or anything.'

Ben studied his coffee cup. 'It's … well, it's family money, I suppose. I don't talk about it.'

And he didn't, so that was that. Bunty, feeling a little chastised, watched a couple walk into the cafe with two small children. The woman was stunning, and Bunty wondered how she'd kept her figure with two kids so small and so close together in age. Ben squinted in her direction too, but she could see that he was looking at the children. How he must miss them. Then without any preamble he said, 'Shall we go for a run?'

He was staring at the woman's tanned legs. Bunty looked at them and then down at her own, which would only have come up to the other woman's knees.

'Sorry?'

'A run. I mean, we keep meeting and eating, don't we?' Ben laughed. 'You must be fit from all that fencing and stuff. How about we meet up for a run tomorrow?'

Bunty paused. Was she going to lie still further? She decided not to. 'I hate running,' she said at length. 'Sorry, but with legs as short as these it's pretty much a given that I was intended to drive everywhere.'

'Well, there's always …' Ben leaned over and stroked one of the offending thighs. 'There's always other exercise.'

Bunty swallowed hard. There was. There was definitely other exercise. And the length of her legs really didn't matter for that. Ben's black eyes were boring into her own; she manoeuvred her way out of the beam and kissed his cheek. 'Soon,' she whispered. God knows she didn't really want to be so coy, but the 'talking about himself' thing was definitely working, and she had to assume that the 'keep him wanting' adage was working too. Weekend, she told herself, nuzzling his earlobe. I'll allow myself to … at the weekend.

It was five days away. Four. A little chat with Ben, looking forward to their next meeting. Three. Two. An early phone call, even before Graham had made it out of the house, where Bunty had been forced to be a bit evasive, and Ben had sounded a bit tense. Or terse. The tone reminded her of something. And then it was the day, D-Day, Drop-em Day as Kat had started to call it. But before she'd even left the house a terrible foreboding had filled her chest cavity. And sure enough, he didn't show up. That was what it had reminded her of – the terseness. It was the tone he'd used when getting worried about the children. As if it were somehow her fault.

At least this time she didn't wait around for hours, hoping. She knew he'd gone. But she blamed herself. Again, and again, and again.

To: buntymckenna@ntsworld.com
From: admin@croesusclub.com
Dear Bunty,
Just to inform you that I have this morning deducted four hundred GBP from your VISA card as the Love Lottery payment. The lovely Ben tells me you have now been on several dates so this is quite within the terms of the agreement.
Yours
Priscilla

To: admin@croesusclub.com
From: buntymckenna@ntsworld.com
Priscilla, you can shove your payment, your Love Lottery, and Lovely Bloody Ben. I have never been so miserable in my life. Well, I have but it was very long time ago. *GIVE ME HIS NUMBER!!!!*
Bunty x

From: admin@croesusclub.com
To: buntymckenna@ntsworld.com
No can do, I'm afraid.
PX

To: admin@croesusclub.com
From: buntymckenna@ntsworld.com
Yeah, well I was joking. Sort of.

From: admin@croesusclub.com
To: buntymckenna@ntsworld.com
I see. Ha ha.

You have now exhausted your three introductions through the Croesus Club. If you wish to meet anyone else there will be a further 300 GBP charge and we will trawl our database again.

Do let me know if you'd like to meet someone new.
Priscilla

From: buntymckenna@ntsworld.com
To: admin@croesusclub.com
I liked the one I'd met. Don't think I can stand any more.
Bye
Bunty x

CHAPTER FIFTEEN

With the energy and direction of a sleepwalker, Bunty ploughed on through the next few days. There seemed to be nothing to do but wait for the inevitable and try to cling on to what vestiges of a normal life she still had. As Kat had told her that she was not, under any circumstances, to trail around wondering what Ben was doing (although, of course, it was nearly impossible to do that), she took to stalking Graham instead. Might as well find out what he was really up to – when he was actually going to be moving Kylie Minogue into their home and asking Bunty to leave.

Sunday strained her nerves until Bunty wanted to weep, but she avoided it, emptied and cleaned her cupboards, and knocked herself out with a bottle of wine until Monday appeared. Everything after school drop-off, which she agreed to for want of anything else to do, seemed likely to be uneventful. She flicked listlessly through the channels, catching snippets of *On the Sofa* with Pearl and Finn, and ordering two different types of Supermodel face creams and an Air-Master Super-Walker that would stow neatly under the bed when not in use and give her buns of steel when it was. Ha. Bloody Kylie had better watch out. She made an over-elaborate healthy lunch for herself and then couldn't be bothered to eat it, so instead she wandered out into the garden and peeked hopefully over the fence. Maybe Mary had a nice pie in the oven or something.

To her immense surprise, and slight chagrin, there was a party going on in Mary's garden. Mallory was regaling Mary with some hilarious tale, at which she squeaked and squealed like a five-year-old at her birthday party. Bunty stared at Mary. She looked exactly the same in every sense, apart from, well … a glow as tangible as a Ready Brek outline. Her aura was practically pulsating. Sex, thought Bunty. She's having sex.

And then she heard another laugh, a fulsome honk, from behind the tree, and there was Dan, beer in hand, stamping his enormous foot on the little patch of ground beneath which Flinders used to lie. 'He's full of rubbish, Mary. Take no notice of him,' he was saying, shaking his head, clearly enjoying the story even more than Mary. 'There,' he continued, stamping one last time, 'no more problems there. I think it was just a bit of residual water backed up from the …'

Bunty coughed. 'You're not going to blame my garden, are you?'

Dan looked up in surprise and then beamed. 'Well, Mrs McKenna. Why aren't you this side of the fence?'

'I was beginning to wonder that myself.'

Mary waved her over and she went to join them at the neat cast iron table. It was an unseasonably warm day, and the sunlight bounced off the golden leaves of the beech trees between their two gardens, suffusing the whole of Mary's patio with a burnished shimmer. How had she not noticed? How had she failed to notice that it was a glorious day and that some kind of festive harvest lunch was taking place just yards from her back door? Ben had a lot to answer for, thought Bunty furiously.

But then she corrected herself. Not Ben. It wasn't his fault that she'd found herself in need of a new husband and had hoped he might turn out to be the one. It was Graham's fault. Graham who was philandering. Creating a vacuum in the 'husband' area of her life.

'I made this,' said Dan proudly, showing her an intricate looking terrine. 'You can have a piece, you know. I do wash my hands.'

'Thank you, I will,' said Bunty primly, and she balanced the pâté and a piece of French bread on her knee, and followed it with a glass of wine and a home-made Madeleine, courtesy of Mary. This was actually nice. Normal. What normal people did when they met up casually of a lunchtime and enjoyed each other's company. It felt refreshingly unforced.

It felt the same when Dan stood up to leave. Realising that Mary and Mallory were getting more and more touchy-feely behind the platter of home-grown radishes (Mallory's, she presumed. They reminded her of Graham's ears.), Bunty got to her feet too. But she didn't want to leave. The afternoon stretched ahead of her with no respite, nothing until Charlotte got home from school, and the thought of … well, thoughts, really, filled her with dread. 'Have you got a job to go to, Dan?' she said lightly. God, did that sound like a proposition? She'd have to keep that flirt gland in check now it had been released.

''Fraid so. Clearing a rat out of a drainpipe two roads over. Seriously.'

Bunty shuffled around for a moment and then blurted, 'Can I come?'

'Sure.' Dan cocked his head on one side for a moment. 'Funny way to spend an afternoon though. Wouldn't you rather stay and have a cup of tea with Mary?' They both looked at Mary, who was laughing so hard and so flirtatiously that her teeth could have been in peril. 'Okay. No. You come with me then. How are you with rotten vermin?'

'Dan, I have plenty of experience,' she said with feeling. 'I'll just put my wellies on.'

She felt ridiculously excited at the prospect of an afternoon in Dan's van, and scampered out of her driveway feeling happier than she had since Ben's last phone call. 'You are seriously strange,' said Dan, seeing her enormous grin.

'Oh, I'm strange?' Bunty slammed the door shut behind her. 'Dan, Dan the Drainage Man makes terrine and cat gravestones in his spare time, and takes his mother to the movies.'

Dan grinned, fluttering his black eyelashes at her. 'Well, you are aware that sticking my hands up people's drains wasn't exactly my first calling. But modelling school was full. And I like helping people.'

Bunty looked at him sideways as his plate-sized hand shoved the van into gear and they juddered around the corner. Help me, Dan, she thought. Could he help her? Right at that moment he looked so enormously capable, so ... big, that she was pretty sure he could lift up the whole planet and rest it on his shoulder like Atlas. Or was it Zeus? Anyway, if he could cope with all that, he could certainly cope with her.

'Graham's having an affair,' she said suddenly.

Dan looked momentarily surprised, and then he nodded. 'I thought there was a strange vibe between you at that dinner party. Have you got proof?'

'He keeps telling me he's playing squash with Ryan.'

'Ryan's got bad knees,' said Dan, in a cruelly accurate impression of Petra. 'Hasn't he?'

'So he's not playing squash.'

'Or working extra late,' offered Dan, taking a guess.

'And I've seen him get out at the squash club and kiss this little blonde chippy with a bottom, no, not a bottom, a derrière, and he said he's going to football –'

'With Ryan?'

'With Ryan. And Ryan did drop him off after this weekend away but there was something weird about it, and they definitely hadn't been to football.'

Dan tapped his fingers on the steering wheel. 'Threesomes with Petra?'

'Nah,' they said together.

'Has he got a bag?' he asked finally, after a few minutes of concentration.

'A bag?'

'Yeah, like a bag he takes everywhere even when he's not likely to need it, with a change of clothes and a bottle of Lynx.'

Bunty paled. 'He has. A shag bag. And new clothes too.'

Dan nodded. 'Then I'm sorry to have to say it, Bunty, but there's your proof. It does sound very much as though your husband is having an affair.' He blew out his cheeks. 'Silly bastard. Are you okay?'

Was she ok? He hadn't actually left her yet, that was true. And she wasn't sick, or dying, and there were people far worse off in the world and all that. But … 'No,' she said quietly. 'Not really.'

Dan nodded slowly. 'Okay. We'll clear this drain. And then you and I are going to do something really fun together.'

'What?' said Bunty, mildly alarmed but more excited than she'd been in quite a few days.

'Spy on Graham,' he said. 'MWAH, ha ha haaaa. Evil genius laugh,' he added by way of explanation.

Bunty couldn't help but smile. 'Look, I'm smiling. Miserable as I am, I'm actually smiling. Dan, you are a very nice man. How come nobody's snapped you up?'

'It would be denying the rest of womankind if I got spliced, wouldn't it? It would have to be a special kind of woman to nail me down these days. One with a very big heart.' And he spread his hands in a 'catch-Kat's-breasts' fashion. 'Yeah. But just because I like to play the field a bit, doesn't mean I approve when a married geezer does it. Especially when they're married to someone as nice as you. We'll sort him, Bunty. Don't you worry.'

She believed him too. True to his word, as soon as they had extracted the decomposing corpse of the rat from the pipe work (which Bunty had to do in the end as her hands were small enough to grab the tail and pull), they piled back into the van, he handed her a cap with his company logo on it, and they set off towards the town centre. 'Where does he work?'

'Coleman Street. Farraday Financial Advisors.'

173

They parked outside for a time, while Dan went in and made spurious claims about the poor drains to the receptionist at Farradays. He emerged ten minutes later, shrugging his door-wide shoulders. 'They have a squash ladder, and guess what? Graham's not on it. And neither's Ryan. But it's coming up for five now, so we can tail him and see where he goes. He won't recognise you in my van.'

'I've got to get home for Charlotte!' Bunty had been so involved in the investigation she'd completely forgotten the one thing she actually had planned that day. 'She can let herself in but she'll be wondering where I am.'

Sure enough, her phone bleeped at that very moment. 'Look, she's missing me.'

She showed him the text. '*Wots 4 t, im starving? & where r u?*'

'*Home in five,*' she tapped in quickly. 'I have to go home, Dan.'

'Sure?' Dan looked immensely disappointed. 'We could pick up young Charlotte and come back.'

'I don't really want her spying on her own father. Although I think he may be playing her off against me already, taking her to meet the derrière woman.'

'Silly, silly bastard.' Dan shook his head again and ferried her home. 'Tell you what,' he said, leaning across to open the passenger door for her, 'you text me when he says he's going out this week, and I'll tail him for you.'

'Yes! And I could come with you if Charlotte's out.' Bunty paused before she closed the door. 'Thanks, Dan. I really appreciate it.'

Dan doffed his cap. 'All part of the service, ma'am.' Mellors. He definitely had a Mellors sort of appeal about him.

Bunty almost skipped inside, feeling more positive than she had in ages. Since the vasectomy letter even. What was that about? As Charlotte opened the door to her, hand on hip as she took in Bunty's flushed face and her clod-covered wellingtons, it came to her. It was a grand gesture. Dan's assistance was a big solid handshake in her direction, a grand gesture that was enabling her to fulfil her own grand gesture. If she could find out what Graham was up to she could confront him with it. Find out why he'd done it. Perhaps, even so, find something to save their marriage? If there was anything left to save. She threw her arms around Charlotte, planted a huge kiss on her cheek, and swept past her up the hallway.

'Mu-um. Mu-ud,' crooned Charlotte behind her.

She'd left a trail of soggy footprints right along the 'deep vanilla' carpet. 'Oh well,' said Bunty airily.

Charlotte's eyes boggled. 'If I'd done that you'd have totally murdered me.'

'That's true,' conceded Bunty. 'But as it was me, and it's my carpet, and I always have to clean it anyway, I'm prepared to live with it. I'll wait till it dries. Cleans up better that way.'

In a funny way, she thought, as she pulled open the freezer door looking for something for dinner, that was like an analogy for her life at the moment. There were muddy marks on the path of their marriage. Was she prepared to live with it? What she was actually doing, she realised, was waiting for it to dry so she could clean it up more easily. Better to sit it out and wait until Graham's affair was over or he actually ended it, than end it herself. Better, even, to have sorted herself out with an alternative for when the crunch time came. It was all just waiting for mud to dry.

But now she felt invigorated. With Dan's help she could get to the bottom of the mystery, face up to Graham with it and take some positive action to sort out the sorry mess that had become her marriage. Her life, in fact. After some more spying.

Next evening, with Kristiana supposedly overseeing Charlotte's homework while Graham 'played squash' and Bunty 'went to the pictures,' she texted Dan as instructed. 'Pick you up in ten minutes,' came the reply.

It was really quite exciting. The date that wasn't a date. The date that was actually, as a matter of fact, rather like espionage. She felt like Pussy Galore, although she didn't imagine that Pussy would have been quite so happy to clamber into a Ford Transit that smelt of a strange mixture of sewage, damp earth, and Jazz aftershave.

It was not a van that pulled up further down the street, however, but a rather smart Alfa Romeo. Dan peeked out from under the visor. 'Well, get in,' he hissed. 'Don't want everybody knowing you're driving around town with strange men, do you?'

'Dan, this is lovely. Did my drainage bill pay for this?'

'No,' said Dan comfortingly. 'But it was the down payment on my TVR.'

There was a lot of money in drains, apparently. They chatted about it as Dan skimmed the roads towards the squash club. 'Let's face it,' said Dan, 'people will always pay more for something they're not prepared to do themselves. And drains affect everyone.'

Bunty blinked. 'Wow. I never thought of that. That's why you take days to turn up. Everyone has drains.'

'They do. Occasional blockages. Pooh and disintegrated sanitary towels spilling out into the garden. And they don't all have Dan, Dan the Drainage Man on hand. I could make an absolute mint if I could clone myself.' Dan pulled into a dark corner of the club car park and dropped the car into neutral. 'Look, is that him?'

'Yes. And he is with Ryan. Weird.'

The men were traipsing out of the squash club, not a racket between them but clearly post-exertion of some kind. Ryan was sporting a spectacularly crotch-grabbing pair of shorts that did his long dangly legs no favours whatsoever, and probably accounted in part for the strange gasping way in which he talked. Graham looked very much more at ease; although he was pink and a little glowing, he had showered so that his fair, tufty hair parted over his ears, and his clean polo shirt hung loosely over his jeans. 'He's lost more weight,' said Bunty. He looked almost fit.

'You do know there's a gym in there as well, don't you?' said Dan.

'No, is there?' It sort of made sense, of course, that a squash club might have other fitness facilities too.

'It's not a very good one, but it's got all the right equipment. And it's bloody cheap.'

'Cheap? It's cheap? Oh, of course!'

Bunty could hardly believe her own stupidity. He was looking fitter because he was getting fitter, because he was going to the gym, the gym with Ryan. And it was cheap. Cheap. That's why they were going to the squash club and not the flash place outside town with a pool and a bar and everything. Because they were a couple of financial advisors! They went for the best financial deal, not the sexiest facilities. And why would he be getting fit? For her! For his own wife! To surprise her with his lean physique and entice her into bed with his dexterous deltoids, and convince her that sex was just for play now as he'd had a vasectomy.

'He's not having an affair at all,' she whispered, wondering why some part of her felt strangely disappointed while the rest of her experienced a surge of elation. 'He's been going to the gym!'

But Dan had thrust the car into gear. 'Let's not count our chickens,' he said. 'Maybe he's been going to the gym *because* he's having an affair. And maybe, Jesus, you don't think it *is* with Ryan like Kat said, do you? Only he's getting into the car with old stringy-legs.'

'Yeah, but it makes sense to share a lift from work, doesn't it?'

'We'll just check, shall we?'

Dan eased out into the fitful traffic, taking advantage of the dusk, and followed Ryan's car. Bunty sat with clenched hands, honestly not knowing whether she wanted Graham to go to work, go directly to work not passing go, not passing affair signs; and then not really knowing why she should have any doubts at all about how glad she should be that her husband was dallying. 'There. Coleman Street,' she said, pointing through the gloom.

Dan followed her finger and then turned to her knowingly. 'He's not turning. Look, they're going straight on. What are you up to, you strange, silly bastard?' he muttered under his breath.

'They're stopping!' squeaked Bunty. 'Pull over, pull over!'

Needing no second bidding, Dan stuck on his left indicator and swerved in behind a parked car. They could just see Ryan's car idling at the kerbstone. 'That's Graham's car,' said Bunty, seeing the dark Mondeo just in front of Ryan's. 'So they parked out here and drove back in together.'

'Why would they do that?' Dan peered around the car in front of them. 'Hang on. Graham's getting out. He's saying goodbye to Ryan. He's moving towards his car. He's getting his hand out of his pocket, he's … '

'Dan, I can see all this. He's … ' Getting into his car, she was about to say, but then Graham swivelled on his heel and approached the door of a tall Georgian house.

'He's knocking on the door. He's smiling. There's a blonde woman. He's kissing her on the cheek. Oh. Now the other cheek. He's going inside. He's closing the door.'

'Dan,' said Bunty. 'Will you shut up?'

'Okay,' said Dan meekly. He looked at her for a long moment, then patted her arm. It was like being belted by an air hammer. 'Home?' he said softly.

Bunty nodded, not daring to speak too soon in case her voice wobbled and gave her away. Home. Whatever that was. She certainly didn't want to hang around until he came out of the house of the blonde again. The Kylie. The … She glared at the metal plaque next to the front door, hoping for a moment that it might say 'counsellor' or 'psychiatrist' or even, weirdly, 'prostitute' but which in fact said 'Verity Reynolds, Media Consultant.'

So there it was. Graham and Verity. Graham and Verity and Charlotte. Happy Christmas from buff Graham and Kylie-ish Verity and my bloody Charlotte who would have to call herself Charlie with Verity Reynolds for a stepmother. 'Home,' she croaked.

She had to bury her nose in her daughter's artfully tousled hair. While there was still time.

CHAPTER SIXTEEN

What the hell was a 'media consultant' anyway? Bunty thought crossly as she slammed the front door behind Graham's retreating back the next morning.

He had come home an hour-and-a-half later than Bunty. Judging by his usual performance that should have been sufficient to copulate perhaps one, one-and-a-half times. To establish the truth, Bunty resorted to giving him a quick sniff, which she turned into a fake sneeze, but he just smelt the same as always. Only when she remembered the shag bag did she figure out why – he was obviously careful to shower before returning home. Unable to meet his eye, Bunty buried herself in Charlotte's homework, with only half-faked parental concern, and then lay in the bath until he was likely to have fallen asleep.

Over breakfast that morning he had watched her with a slightly wary eye, as though he was expecting trouble. Well, let him, she thought. It was all right for him with his Verity Reynolds and his newly honed physique. Where was her Ben when she needed him? She'd not even had sex and she felt more guilty than Graham clearly did. Finally, as she banged her way through the creation of Charlotte's vegan packed lunch wondering if one large carrot would suffice as she hadn't bothered shopping for anything else, he ventured to speak.

'I'm going to be home by six tonight.'

'Ooooh! Lucky us,' said Bunty, thrusting Charlotte's lunch box into her backpack.

'Um. Shall I bring home some dinner? Chinese?'

'If you like.'

'I thought we could eat it in front of the TV. There's a good financial programme on at seven thirty.'

Bunty paused. Was that what he did with Verity Reynolds? Chinese and a viewing of some financial programme. It hardly seemed likely, and she was suddenly incensed at the unfairness of it all. Verity Reynolds would get keen and clean Graham, trying-hard Graham, look-at-my-new-abs Graham, and then he'd come 'home' to them and they'd get bloody takeaways and the same old drone on the TV. How dare he? How absolutely dare he?

'Graham, I can hardly wait,' she said with ill-concealed venom.

The first thing she did when left on her own was to make like Charlotte and head for the computer. It was a shame that Graham had taken his laptop with him; it would have been interesting to see how quickly Verity Reynolds popped up in the drop-down list of histories. Pulling herself in close to the computer, Bunty tentatively typed 'V' into the Google bar. She was immediately greeted by the list from hell – Vanya, Vagina, Vigina ... 'Oh my God!' she shrieked, smacking the 'delete history' button, and hastily adding an 'e' to the existing 'V.' Nothing. Even when she'd typed in the whole of the name Verity, there was nothing obvious on the search engine, apart from one Verity Lambert who had been something to do with *Doctor Who*. That was media, wasn't it? She was old, though, Bunty noticed when looking at the dates. Dead, in fact. Definitely not the Verity she was looking for.

Only when she'd typed in 'Verity Reynolds Media Consultant' did the computer produce any results. Verity, it seemed, offered a broad portfolio of media services ('Bet she does,' snarled Bunty. 'Phone sex. Internet sex. Got them all covered, hey, Verity?') There was a professional-looking photograph of a pert blonde with a long bob and an expensively veneered smile, and then a list of credits which, to Bunty's amazement, featured *On the Sofa* with Pearl and Finn among other TV shows. What did she do with them? Bunty reached for her phone.

'Kat, what does a media consultant do?' In her employment services role, Kat was bound to know.

'Oh, a range of things,' said Kat. 'It can be advertising, selling media space, buying media space, PR, writing press releases. I think I've got a junior role coming up if you're interested.'

'Course I'm not interested!' Bunty wished she could pour the image of Verity Reynolds down the phone to her friend. 'I've found the woman that Graham's been seeing. She's a media consultant. Verity Reynolds.'

'Right,' said Kat, 'let me ask some people and I'll get back to you. Have to be before tonight, of course.' And she let out an excited '*Yes!*'

'What's happening tonight?'

Kat tutted loudly. 'Uh, I'm leaving, on a jet plane, don't know when I'll be back again. Not that you'd care.'

'Oh God. You're going to see Simon. I'm so sorry, Kat, I forgot.' Bunty finished with a sigh. She'd been so wrapped up in her own domestic dramas that she'd completely forgotten that her friend was looking forward to meeting up with her own Kiwi man. An image of Ben flitted into her mind and she pushed it to one side. 'Do you want a lift to the airport?'

'Oh, that's all right,' said Kat. She always forgave her friends so easily. 'Dan's dropping me off.'

'Dan? My Dan? I mean, Dan, Dan the drainage man?' Alarm bells clanged in Bunty's head. How many Dans did Kat know? Was she going straight from one man to the other? Was everybody in the world – across the world – at it?

'The very same, although I like to think of him as Dan, Dan, with the very big … van. I need the space. For my luggage,' said Kat. 'I'll miss you though.'

'Me too. Give my love to Cally.'

'Right. And I'll call you back if I hear anything about Veronica Ronald.'

'Verity Reynolds.'

'Right. Big hugs from the big jugs.'

'Kat, you are *gross*,' said Bunty, in a pretty good imitation of Charlotte, so that they were both laughing as they put down the phone. Gaaad, she was going to miss that woman, particularly right now when she needed her friends around. Both her best mates on the other side of the globe. It wasn't fair. Nothing was very bloody fair at the moment.

And talking of not fair, time for a bit more stalking. Bunty drove across town in a dream, a mental version of some form of

184

Beauty and the Geek playing through her head, where Graham (geek) had to choose between Bunty and Verity (beauties – well, relatively anyway) and Kat ummed and aahed with her finger on her pouty lips between Simon and Dan, and Verity, somehow, wrote press releases about the whole thing for the TV pages of the *Evening Standard*. Before she knew it, she was driving up Verity's road and pulling up just near her house.

She ducked down behind the steering wheel. Quite what she'd intended to do once she got her, Bunty wasn't at all sure. This was what they'd do on a programme, wasn't it? Turn up at the house. Confront the lover. Maybe punch her in the face? Bunty shuddered. Violence still didn't come naturally to her, no matter how satisfying it looked on TV. She closed her eyes. What was she doing here? What could she possibly achieve by turning up at the home (office?) – home stroke office – of her husband's mistress and sitting outside her house, other than working herself up into an impossible frenzy, which she would probably, let's face it, take out on Charlotte.

Tap tap tap.

Bunty's eyes flew open. She had slumped so far down behind the wheel that her chin was on her chest. She swivelled her eyes right. Crouching down on a level with her was the beaming face of Verity Reynolds, so close that Bunty could see the artfully applied false eyelashes, adding depth to the corners of almond-shaped eyes, which were a rather startling shade of green. Fake, thought Bunty. Fake eyelashes. Fake corneas. Even the bottom was probably fake – a pair of those wonder tights with false buttocks shoved in them so everybody could get a Beyoncé Bum just by dragging on their fishnets. Verity Reynolds' arse was probably as flat as her exercised belly.

Tap tap tap. Verity was signing madly for Bunty to wind down the window. That involved switching the engine on, and as Bunty had temporarily forgotten her own name, she opened the door instead, pulled it to quickly in case Verity Reynolds intended to punch her first, then opened it again.

'Are you my ten thirty?' Verity Reynolds had the voice of a newscaster, somewhere between headmistress and just plain mistress.

'Your what?'

The woman consulted the Blackberry in her hand. So she even knew how to use one of those. Bitch. 'Ten thirty. Susie Williams. Sell your house in thirty minutes.'

Was that an order? Did she already have designs on her goddamn house? 'I ... I don't want to sell my house.'

Verity opened her beautiful mouth and laughed right down a full octave, like someone running their finger across a piano keyboard. 'Ha ha ha ha ha ha haaaa. No, silly. You're not Susie Williams then.'

'No, I'm Bun ... Buh ... Benito.' Oh crap. Mussolini. That must be the man version. 'Benita.'

'Oh. Love. I could help with that stammer,' said Verity sympathetically, laying a manicured hand across the top of the door. Bunty resisted the temptation to slam the door shut. 'But if you're not Susie at ten thirty, then she's a bit late, but she might turn up so I'd have to pencil you in for another date. Here's my card. Sorry to disturb.'

186

She waggled her fingers at Bunty with a cheery grin and disappeared back in the house. Bunty stared after her, bewildered. What had just happened? She thought she was about to be set upon by her husband's lover but instead she'd arranged to meet up with her to deal with her non-existent stammer. And … and … and, oh Christ, maybe she did have a stammer, she thought, as her ideas failed to gather themselves into any coherent pattern. And Verity Reynolds was … nice. She couldn't be nice. She wasn't allowed to be nice. Bunty did not want anything about her competition to be nice at all. She wanted to hate her. Instead, she could almost see what Graham would see in her, apart from the obvious prettiness (fake as it was); VR seemed efficient, and friendly, and sort of … energetic. If she had kids, and she obviously didn't, she'd run the PTA with her left hand while media consulting with her right, and still manage to look 'Stunning in Something Simple' at the fundraiser while Little Verity and Veritas ran the fruit-juice stand.

Hmm. Maybe she did hate her after all.

But overall, it wasn't fair. It just wasn't fair at all. And there was someone else pulling up in a nifty little Nissan Figaro, similarly highlighted, pony-toothed and pony-tailed, and swishing up to Verity Reynolds' front door and doing that whole 'mwah mwah, dahling' air-kissing then tossing her head around while she apologised for being late. It was a clone. A Verity Reynolds clone. Good God, was Graham involved in some sort of *Stepford Wives* perfect-woman creation plan?

187

'Calm down, Bunty!' She really had to get a grip on her imagination. Nonetheless, the meeting with VR, the in-her-face evidence that Graham was looking for something else, brought home an untidy collection of realisations. One, she wasn't enough for Graham any more. Two, if even she found someone to be attractive because they were efficient and energetic, why wouldn't your average red-blooded male? And three, if she didn't even come up to par for Graham, no wonder Ben had lost interest. 'He'd love Verity Reynolds too,' she thought mournfully. Someone in charge of her life. Someone vivacious. Fun. Rather like Bunty used to be.

And she put her head on the steering wheel and sobbed, not for Ben, or for Graham, but for the person she used to be, with dreams and expectations, and a *joie de vivre* which seemed to have disappeared into the drainage system along with Flinders. Everyone around her seemed to be moving on – Graham, for sure; but Cally too, and now Kat. And pretty soon even Charlotte would be leaving home, off to university, or nannying in America, or Club Med waitressing in Europe, or … *something* interesting. While she, Bunty McKenna, had not even managed to set herself up successfully with a new husband for when the existing one dumped her. She had failed, as a wife, maybe as a mother, perhaps even as a person. She had failed in life. F on her score card. A big fat F.

As her sobbing eased, Bunty lifted her head. She was still outside Verity Reynolds' house, with make-up like Alice Cooper and no suitable reason for being there. Enough, she decided. Feeling a little better after wailing like a small child for a good few minutes, she rammed the Mini into gear and set off on a trip around town. Enough. She had moped and circumnavigated, and reacted to the negative and not the positive. Enough. A new plan was needed. A positive one. 'ENOUGH ALREADY!' she screamed out of the sun roof, feeling alive again for the first time in ages. She was going to take control. She might even get in touch with Priscilla again.

As if reading her mind, her phone rang.

A New Zealand number. 'Hello,' she said cautiously. It might be Cally. Or it might not.

'Do you absolutely hate me? I wouldn't blame you,' said a deep voice.

Bunty pulled over instantly, shaking her head in disbelief. Wasn't it always the way? Just as she'd decided to move on, do something new, the man who'd disappeared, 'Mr Ten Days On and Ten Days Off', had decided to rear his not-so-ugly head again. 'Ben. What a surprise.'

'I know, I know.' He sounded slightly drunk. 'I piked on you again, and yet you're still talking to me. I'm so sorry. I just got into a hard time over the kids again, and I couldn't face talking to anyone, especially – forgive me for this – especially someone who's kind of going through the same thing.' Ben sighed, then hiccuped.

'Right. So you had to go into your cave.' Bunty couldn't even be mad about it really. She'd read all the 'Men are off this planet' books like everybody else, and it was true – men did retreat with their problems. Graham's answer was to retreat to the study with the *Financial Times* and a spreadsheet package. Or at least it had been before the cave turned into an attractive Georgian terrace on the other side of town. Ben, on the other hand, clearly took refuge in the bottle.

'Are you looking after yourself, Ben?' she said softly. 'It's not even eleven o'clock and you sound like … like you've had a few.

'I have had a few,' said Ben. He sounded quite proud of the fact. 'She can't tell me what to do any more, can she? So I've had as much as I want. Sun's up over the yardarm and all that.'

The sun's up … didn't that mean it was evening. Bunty drew in a breath. 'Ben, where are you?'

'I'm in the –,' he paused to gulp down a belch, 'marina in Auckland. Back in New Zealand. That's the other reason I didn't get in touch. I didn't really want to say goodbye, you know?'

So he had gone. Bunty gulped herself, fighting down the lump that had appeared in her throat. So much for a new plan. The old one took a bit of beating. 'You left?'

Ben sounded close to tears. 'I had to get the boat back. And the kids … she was threatening all sorts. I had to get back. But I … I do miss you, Bunty. I think we could have really had something. If we just lived a bit closer.'

'I … think so too.'

'Is it okay if I call you? I could be back soon. We could … you know.'

Actually she didn't know. Finally shag? Pick up where they left off? Fall in love, get married, have their own children … Any of those sounded very appealing. Hell, all of those sounded very appealing. 'Ben, what if …'

A soft snort stopped her in her tracks. 'Ben. Wake up. Wake up, Ben,' she called. 'Ben!'

But the snoring continued. He sounded adorable. Like a puppy. Bunty smiled and hit the 'end call' button, a bubble of anticipation rising in her chest.

So here was the new plan. Her own grand gesture. Fingers crossed it would work and she too could move on, get her happy ending. Bunty speed-dialled her number one number. 'Kat, can Dan pick me and Charlotte up too?'

'Awww,' wailed Kat, overcome with bonhomie. 'Are you coming to see me off? Sweeeeeet!'

'Bugger that,' said Bunty, her heart starting to race. 'We're coming with you.'

CHAPTER SEVENTEEN

The last time Bunty and Kat had travelled across the world, Bunty had left Charlotte behind with Graham. She was already beginning to regret not doing the same this time.

It was really not the same as when Charlotte was a little girl. Before the age of five she could have whisked Charlotte away without a moment's thought, as long as she had enough food and clothes for a couple of weeks. Now it meant protracted negotiation with her school, her grandparents, and with Charlotte herself. She'd approached the school first.

Bunty: I'd like to take Charlotte out of school for few weeks.

School Secretary: How many's a few?

Bunty: I don't know exactly.

SS: Anything up to two weeks is frowned upon but you might just get away with it depending on the circumstances. More than two weeks needs an application in triplicate up to three years beforehand, and then there's no guarantee we'll keep your child's place open. More than one month is tantamount to child abuse, frankly.

Bunty: Okay, it'll just be two weeks then.

SS: Circumstances?

Bunty: Family emergency.

SS: Death of a family member?

Bunty: Yes.

That was more or less how the conversation had gone, and with threats of Social Services and Truancy officers hanging over her head, Bunty signed Charlotte out of school for two weeks – which ran into half term, thereby affording them three weeks if they needed it. If she decided just to stay away, she doubted the education authority would be bothered to send an officer to New Zealand.

Her parents, however, were a different matter, although the conversation had run very much along the same lines.

'I'm thinking of going to New Zealand for a couple of weeks.'

'How many?'

'Don't know.'

'What about Charlotte's school? They don't like you taking them out for more than a week or so now, you know.'

'I know.'

'Over two weeks and she'll be off down the mall in one of those hooded outfits robbing old people.'

'I don't think Charlotte would do that, Mum.'

'You'd be surprised. It's what young people do these days. What about Graham?'

'I don't think he'd do it either.'

'Bunty. You know what I mean. What about his work?'

'He's not coming.' In fact, he doesn't even know we're going and he won't be given the option to join us but he should have thought about that before entering the den of Verity Reynolds, she nearly added, but thought better of it. 'And we're off in a couple of hours, so I'd better get packing.'

'Oh. We were going to come round to see you tonight. Graham invited us.'

Graham invited them? Probably the time he was going to break it to everyone that he was leaving. 'Well, don't bother, because we won't be there.'

'All right, darling. I'm sure you know what you're doing,' finished her mother in a tone that suggested completely the opposite. 'We'll see you when you get back.'

And then there'd been Charlotte herself.

'Why are we going? Tonight? Why tonight? I don't want to go. I've got orchestra this weekend. I hate flying. How long? I *hate* flying. Hang on. Will Paige be there? Can I forget about social sciences homework? Can we go now? Come *on*, Mum.'

Ever since Bunty had picked her up after school and broken the news to her she had vacillated in a similar fashion, and twelve hours later, on the plane, she was still doing so.

'Am I allowed to watch that? Why not? Everyone at school has seen it, like, twice. Can I? Can I watch it? Oh you're totally *mean*. What's that? That looks good. Can I watch that? That thing that you're watching. What is it? What's it about? Well, if it's right in the middle there's no point in watching it now, is there. Can I watch the other thing? Please? Why not?'

It was a war of attrition. Bunty, wired from the madness of the thing she had done and from eating a curry omelette of some kind at 2 a.m., was going to lose. She knew it. Any minute now she would scream, 'WATCH WHAT THE FUCK YOU WANT AND SEE IF I CARE!' down the plane, and the two truancy officers parked neatly at the back in matching suits like the FBI would take an aisle each and surround her with guns. She'd be towed away and locked in the toilet until they landed in

Singapore, and everyone knew what it was like in Singapore – you couldn't chew gum let alone swear at your own offspring.

'Breathe,' said Kat. She was sitting across the aisle, two rows back, as that was the nearest to 'sitting together' they'd been able to get. 'In. And out. That's good, Bun.'

'How did you know?' whispered Bunty across the sleeping Singaporean families.

'Your elbows looked very tense.'

'God, Kat. What have I done?'

Kat gestured to the little space near the toilets, grabbed her newly filled plastic glass of wine and Bunty's, and squeezed her way down the aisle. Bunty checked on Charlotte, now happily watching some Disney film for six-year-olds, made toilet signals and followed Kat.

'So tell me again,' said Kat, leaning on the wall of the hostess station. 'What did you tell Graham?'

'I left him a note. A note! God, how mean. At least he was going to tell me in person. He'd organised a family gathering to pass the news on – my mum said. And Charlotte.'

'And the note said …'

Bunty sighed and repeated it all in one long breath. 'Seeing-as-you're-leaving-me-anyway-I'm-going-with-Kat-to-find-a-nice-Kiwi-man-and-Charlotte's-coming-too-I'll-be-in-touch.'

She tried to imagine Graham's face when he read it, but couldn't. Maybe he'd be pleased. She might have made life very easy for him, leaving the marital home. 'Maybe I should have consulted a lawyer first,' she said.

'And what does Charlotte think you're doing?'

'Getting some me-time with Cally and Paige.'

'And really you're going to track down a man called Ben who has a yacht. In Auckland. Otherwise known as the City of Sails.'

Bunty groaned. 'I'm completely mad, aren't I?'

'Yes,' said Kat, slamming her drink into Bunty's. 'It's fantastic!'

'So … does that mean you'll help me?'

'Try stopping me. After I've caught up with Simon for a few days.' Kat waggled her eyebrows salaciously and staggered back to her seat.

Bunty dropped into her seat next to Charlotte, who was now snuffling gently into her triangular flight pillow (which she'd insisted on buying in Boots at the airport along with travel wipes, a personal fan, super-tight socks to prevent thromboses, and a panoply of other expensive objects that would be of absolutely no use from the second they got off the plane). Charlotte looked adorable when she was asleep, with her face clean of its usual half-scowl and her long lashes lying baby-like on her cheek. Three in the morning their time. Or was that New Zealand time. Whatever. Somewhere in the world it was three in the morning, and that was certainly time to get some sleep …

Pearl: So Bunty, what was going through your mind when you kidnapped your child and absconded twelve thousand miles to meet up with a man you barely knew?

Finn: And were you aware of the police chase going on behind you?

Bunty: No, I …

Pearl (*shuffling her papers and shoving her glasses back up her nose. Stern*). You were aware, of course, that it was illegal to take your child out of school.

Bunty: Not illegal, just sort of …

Finn: Tell us about Ben. What did you know about him?

Bunty: He … he owned a yacht. I met him through some introduction agency called the Croesus Club.

Pearl: That's right, while you were still married.

Finn: Are there clubs for that sort of thing?

Bunty: No, I wasn't married. Well, yes, technically I was, but it was over, or going to be over very soon, and Ben was so lovely and warm, and I needed him.

Pearl (*bristling*): Is that true, Bunty? Or do you think you were just bored out of your mind and needed to create a bit of drama in your life?

Finn: Nobody would blame you for that. Lots of us are bored. Not me, obviously (*flashing toothy grin direct to camera*).

Bunty: No! I don't think … I don't know … You're confusing me. Stop it, Pearl! Stop it!

She woke up with a start, half-afraid that she'd been screaming 'Stop it' down the length of the plane. The only person she'd woken, however, was Charlotte, who was glaring at her from over her eye-mask like a sleep-deprived surgeon. 'I wasn't doing anything. I was *asleep*, in case you hadn't noticed,' she said, her voice oddly muffled by the mask.

'Sorry, darling. Was I telling you to stop it?'

'Well, du-uh.'

197

'Bad dream. Sorry. Go back to sleep.' And no more sleeping for me, ever, like bloody Macbeth, she thought crossly. So she felt guilty for disappearing without a showdown with Graham. Why should she? He'd started it.

Five-and-a-half films, one short stopover in Singapore and several tussles with Charlotte later, they landed in Auckland. Bunty peered back down the plane; Kat had risen like Boudica from the depths of her wine-induced coma, refreshed and lovely with a tumble of wild blonde curls and a dirty smile on her face. By contrast, Bunty felt wizened and dehydrated; she had probably shrunk two sizes and would be about to greet Cally as if she were dressed in her mum's clothes.

But Cally didn't care, even though she'd had to get up at 4.30 a.m. to meet them on time. Bunty returned her enormous squeeze. 'I'm so sorry to land on you like this, with hardly any warning. And at this time of the morning!'

'Bunty, I'm thrilled that you're here. And 4.30 a.m. is a lie-in at the moment. Here's David.' And she pushed forward a buggy with a ten-month-old boy gurning cheerfully from its folds. 'Pete's moving the car. And Paige is just coming … Paige! Help Charlotte with her things, will you?'

'She's got rather a lot,' said Bunty apologetically. Both mothers watched the meeting of Paige and Charlotte with interest. It had been well over a year since they'd seen each other, and email communication, no matter how rude, was no substitute for the real thing; they still stood formally, staring at each other warily like soldiers across no-man's land. Then Paige said, 'I've got the day off school.'

'Yay!' said Charlotte. 'Me too. Well, more like two weeks.'

'Awesome!' said Paige. 'And our school holidays start tomorrow so I'm off too! Yayah!'

And after gawping at each other with awe at their own brilliance, Paige grabbed Charlotte's wheeled case and started off across the concourse, saying, 'I love that pillow thing. What movies did you see on the plane? Did you? Awesome!'

Watching their giggling, retreating backs, Bunty linked arms with Cally. 'And that's the last we'll see of them for two weeks. Or however long …'

'However long it takes to find this man,' said Cally, turning to watch a cuddly figure emerge from the customs area among a mountain of suitcases. 'Oh, there's Kat! Why did she take so much longer than you?'

'Customs kept asking her questions,' said Bunty with a grin. 'She had so much luggage they though she was importing it to open a shop. Oh. There's Simon, I guess.'

She'd only seen Simon briefly before, when he'd been in Fiji chasing after Cally, but from the way he was striding purposefully towards Kat she imagined that the tall, blond man could be no other. When Kat threw her arms around him and kissed him like there was no other oxygen in the room, she knew for sure.

'That's Simon,' agreed Cally. 'I'll see if I can get her to put him down long enough to say hello.'

It took several minutes, but finally Cally managed to greet Kat and arrange to meet up with them in a couple of days when

Kat's 'shag fest' was waning, and then they burst out through the sliding doors into the brittle sheen of a spring morning.

Auckland.

She'd made it.

To Ben.

CHAPTER EIGHTEEN

'I don't know how you do it,' said Bunty to Cally as they slurped coffee out of pudding bowls at a cafe in Mission Bay. The water lapped at the edge of the beach about a hundred yards away across the road, the sun dappling one slope of the volcano that stuck out of the sea a few miles out. Charlotte, sniggering at the next table with Paige, had already decided they would do a day trip out to Rangitoto. Not every day she got to stare down a volcano.

'What?' Cally's face disappeared momentarily behind her coffee cup. Bowl. 'Live here? I know, it's awful, isn't it?'

Bunty grinned. 'I don't mean that. I mean keeping up with appearances. You've just had a baby and look better than you have in years. Mind you, everyone around here looks sickeningly healthy. And gorgeous.' Verity Reynolds and Susie Williams would fit right in, it appeared.

'That's how I do it,' said Cally, nodding at two jogging mothers as she hauled David onto her lap and fed him her biscotti. 'Nothing like a bit of competition to stimulate the 'let's get moving' gene. Although to be honest, I'm not very good at it. It's just life keeping me thin at the moment.' In addition to being a new mum to David, an old mum to Paige and a partner to Pete, Cally had managed to score herself a rather plum job as events co-ordinator for the city's arts foundation. She didn't seem to take it too seriously, though, and still found time to stick around to keep Bunty company, and organise day trips for the days she and Pete wouldn't be around.

Bunty breathed in, a heady concoction of excellent coffee, brine and relaxation. This had been a good choice, she thought, watching the pert behinds of the mother-joggers fade into the distance. Charlotte was having an amazing time catching up with Paige, and loved the house, the pool, the city, the scenery and everything else around with unprecedented hyperbole. 'Wicked!' was definitely her word of the week, closely followed by 'awesome'. Bunty, too, once the jetlag had subsided and she felt as though her legs were her own once more, was beginning to feel the tension slide from her shoulders as the sun played on her skin. It was a therapeutic place, and she was loving it.

Nonetheless, the aim of her mad mission played on her mind, and she dared to raise it again at dinner that evening, when Kat and Simon finally reappeared and they could all crowd around Pete and Cally's pitted pine table.

'Cally, that was fantastic,' she said, pushing her plate away.

'All Pete's doing.' Cally bumped hips with Pete in the open-plan kitchen where they were starting to load the dishwasher. 'His pasta is always amazing.'

Pete smiled evenly. 'After thirty years of feeding myself I know what to do with a handful of spaghetti and a bit of sauce.'

'I bet you do,' growled Kat in her sleaziest voice. Bunty watched over her glass as Simon laughed, shaking his head, and squeezed Kat's fingers across the table. They were very different in so many ways, but for now it seemed to work.

'Talking of which, well, not what you do with spaghetti, but you know, um …' Bunty ran out of ways to introduce the topic she most wanted to discuss. 'Ben,' she said simply, having first checked that Charlotte and Paige were well out of the way, and not on a computer.

Cally wiped her hands on a tea towel and filled all their glasses, raising her eyebrows at Kat. 'Yes. Ben. Tell us what you know about him and we'll see how you can track him down.'

'I know it sounds ridiculous,' said Bunty, 'but I did feel such a connection. He's got issues and baggage and everything, but then haven't we all? You guys all did, and look how it's worked out for you.' There were so many triangles in the relationships of Pete, Cally, Simon and Kat that it was practically a Toblerone. 'I just want to find him. Show him that I can be there for him. Let him feel loved and wanted.'

'And how do you find him?' asked Pete.

'I've got this number for him,' she said, showing him her mobile. 'I've tried calling but there's no reply. I think it may be turned off or run out of power or something. Is that a local number?'

Pete angled his reading glasses and read the little screen on the phone. 'That's a mobile. Could be anywhere. Sorry, Bunty. Do have his surname?'

'He did tell me his surname, but it was so long and complicated that I didn't get it, and I didn't want to ask him again.'

'Maori?' said Cally.

'Or Polynesian,' suggested Simon.

'That's more likely if it was very long,' said Pete. 'But that's not much to go on either.'

Kat sat up brightly. 'He owns a yacht though. Let's go to all the yachtie places.'

'There are quite a few of those, though, Kat,' said Cally.

Kat was not to be defeated, however. 'Okay. We'll start with the biggest and work our way down. It was a big yacht, wasn't it, Bun?'

'I never saw it.' Bunty almost shuddered. She'd never seen it. What must they think of her, coming all this way with so little information? It was madness, but they were all helping her. 'But I suppose so.'

Cally and Pete were looking at each other in a way that Bunty couldn't quite understand, but then Pete said, 'Right, then we start at the Viaduct. Tomorrow's Sunday. It'll be a good day to ask around.'

'And we can fit in a trip from there for the girls,' said Cally. 'I'll take them off to Rangitoto, if you like, while you go Ben-hunting.'

Bunty felt like crying, so grateful was she for all their help. For getting it so completely. For realising how unkind Graham had been, and how Ben could rectify things. She leaned over and gave Cally a hug. 'Thank you for understanding.'

And Cally gave her a kiss on the cheek. 'I'm not really understanding, Bun, if I'm honest, but I am supporting. Like you've done for me. That's what friends are for.'

Kat's eyes had misted over. 'Friends,' she said breathily, clunking her glass against Bunty's then Cally's. 'The three musketeers.'

'Friends,' said Cally and Bunty together.

Bunty took a slug of her drink, playing over in her head what Cally had just said. 'Supporting' was different to 'understanding', it was true. It was what she and Kat had done when they turned up in Fiji for Cally's wedding to Alan, Pete's son, even though they both felt it was a mistake and he wouldn't be right for Cally at all. Now, seeing her with Pete, it was completely evident that it would have been far from just 'not right'. It would have been a disaster.

But that wasn't the same in this case. They didn't like Graham, for a start. Either of them. They'd always thought he was too dull for Bunty, too organised for Bunty, a bit too 'steady Eddie' for Bunty.

And they hadn't even met Ben yet. They'd love him. Just as she could. Even their names went together better. Ben and Bun. Ben and Bun for dinner tonight, darling! Oh, great, they're fun! Ben and Bun. Lots of fun. Ben and Bun on the sofa. Ben and Bun, and Charlotte plus one …

'Bunty!'

'Hmmm?'

'You'd gone completely,' said Cally with a grin. 'Jet lag does that to you. Takes you by surprise.'

Kat faked an enormous yawn. 'Oh, yes, it's got me too. I think we should be heading home to bed, Si. Big day tomorrow.'

'Your wish is my command.' Simon pulled out her chair and slipped her shawl around her shoulders. Honestly, thought Bunty, the man was straight out of the eighteenth century. And Kat lapped it up.

A few minutes later she fell into Cally's spare bed herself, barely seconds after making sure that Charlotte was tucked up in the spare single in Paige's room. Both girls were fast asleep, all talked out. Bunty felt a little talked out herself. But it was a big day tomorrow. The day to find Ben. She sank into a deep sleep, at ease for the first time in months.

Sunday's dawn heralded another bright morning, but even before breakfast was over a bank of ominous grey clouds had smothered the sun.

'Four seasons in one day,' quoted Pete, squinting at the sky. 'We'd better take our raincoats down to the Viaduct.'

'You're coming with me, pal,' said Cally quickly. 'We can drop Bunty off and then you can come to Rangitoto. I'm not climbing a volcano with David on my back.'

'Well, I can't, I'm old,' said Pete, a half-smile playing across his tanned face.

'Nice try,' said Cally. 'We'll take the buggy. Get you in training for your Zimmer Frame.'

Pete looked so far from a Zimmer Frame that they all laughed. Mallory. Now that was old. Bunty watched her friends with a peculiar pang of nostalgia. What was going on at home, she wondered. But then she cast the thought from her mind. This was an important day. A red letter day. And the letter was B.

Simon had opted out of Ben hunting, preferring to get some work done while Kat helped her friend on her sleuthing trip, so after lunch they met up at Viaduct Harbour, ignoring the occasional chilly spray that swept over them, and strode along the jetty checking out yachts.

'Wow. There is quite a lot of them, isn't there?' said Kat, leaning over the balustrade to stare in at one particularly gleaming example. 'Excuse me,' she called to the man clad in shorts and flip-flops who appeared out of the cabin. 'Are you Ben?'

Bunty shoved her to one side. 'Of course he's not Ben. I can tell you if it's Ben or not. Sorry,' she called, pointing to Kat's head. 'Sunstroke.'

'You have to wear your hat here, love,' the man shouted back. 'There's a big hole in the ozone layer right over your head.'

'Thank you.' Kat rolled her eyes at Bunty. 'Maybe he knows Ben. Ask him. Ask him!'

'I can't!'

'But how else are you going to find him?'

It did seem pretty hopeless. Bunty didn't even know what Ben's yacht was called. 'We're .... we're looking for Ben who owns a yacht,' she called feebly, her words seeming to take ages to float down to the man on the boat. 'Which ones are yachts?'

The man's face split into a grin. 'Ninety percent of these are yachts, love. Sail or engine?'

'I ... I don't know.'

'Let me guess. Ben – he's youngish, good-looking, broad-shoulders?'

'Yes!' yelled Bunty. 'That's him.'

'It's half the blokes here, you mean. Sorry, love. Why don't you try the Americas Cup guys?'

He pointed back along the wharf to the restaurant where they'd met for lunch. A pair of musicians were unloading electric acoustic guitars and amplifiers from the back of an SUV. 'The guitar guys?'

At this the man on the boat threw his head back and laughed uproariously. 'The yachties. Out the front. NZL 40 and 41.'

'I don't like him, he's rude,' said Kat. 'How are we supposed to know what he's blathering about?'

Bunty sighed. 'I suppose I should have had a better idea. I didn't really talk to Ben about his yacht. We discussed his children and his ex more, really.'

'Fun.' Kat peered down the wharf. 'Look, there are some people on that boat, and it says NZL 40 on the sail thingy. That must be what he meant.'

They hurried back towards the restaurant, Bunty peeking over the railings at intervals to see if she could spot Ben. There was no way down to the men beavering away on the deck of the yacht, so they raced around the corner to the woman decked out in sailing gear at the top of the steps.

'Are you on this next trip, ladies?' The chipper young woman pointed down the stairs to NZL 40.

'We just want to talk to those men,' said Bunty, suddenly aware that she was ten years older than this woman, and possibly fifteen years older than the crew. 'I don't mean ...'

'Yes, we're going on,' said Kat firmly. 'Put it on my credit card.' They waited while the woman swiped Kat's card, then slithered down the metal steps to the boat. 'Sorry, Bunty, but she was rude too. Did you see the way she was looking at us, like we were some … some sad old clichés or something. Pumas. Eugh! Well, we are not explaining ourselves to her. And this way we have …' Kat checked her itinerary. 'We have two whole hours to interrogate these guys.'

'Good thinking.' Bunty steadied herself as they climbed aboard the yacht just as a squall sent a swell under it. 'And anyway, it's, like, a touristy thing. And we're tourists, aren't we?'

'Too right,' said Kat. She certainly looked like one, in her Auckland Sky Tower cap, Maori design t-shirt, white linen trousers and strappy wedges.

Bunty caught one of the sailors giving Kat the once-over, and not in a positive way. At least dressed in jeans and boots and the raincoat Pete had suggested, she looked the part. Marginally, at least. The man waved them forward. 'Bags and wallets and anything that might get in the way up at the front here, ladies.'

Kat clutched her bag to her. 'It's got my camera in it.'

'You can keep your camera with you, just no handles and things to snag on the equipment. Do you have a camera in yours, ma'am?' he continued to Bunty.

'Just my phone,' she said. 'I'll turn it off.'

As Kat scrabbled around beneath the front mast trying to find the best place for her bag, Bunty paused. One last time, she decided, and she pressed the 'call' button on the New Zealand number that Ben had last called on. There was a loud crackling as usual, and she was about to switch it off when a man's voice said, 'Hello.'

'Ben? Ben, it's …'

Whoever it was, and it didn't sound like Ben, carried straight on. 'Hello, Bin's … Sitting …'

They couldn't hear her. 'Ben? Ben!'

But the crackling resumed and then stopped. The connection was as dead as it had ever been. Bunty felt like crying with frustration, but the young, broad-shouldered, good-looking guy in front of her was saying, 'Phones away, ladies, we're casting off in one minute. Life jackets buckled, please.'

Bunty thrust her bag next to Kat's under the overhang beneath the sail, a little lip of the roof that covered the cabin. 'Someone answered,' she said to Kat as they took up their places down one side of the boat.

'Ben? Was it him? Where is he?'

'It went dead again.'

'Oh God. Oh shit. Shit, shit, shit.'

Bunty smiled. 'It's not that bad. I've got his number now.'

It obviously was that bad, though, as Kat's face had gone white. 'No. I've just realised something. There aren't any seats.'

Bunty looked around. There were definitely no seats. Crew. Big winch-type wheels. Other passengers. But no seats.

'I thought they'd take us into that cabin thing, and we could sit and have a gin and tonic and talk to the men,' said Kat, her eyes round with horror, 'but they're not going to do that, are they? We're up here, in this awful weather, and … omigod we're taking off … aagh! And it's just us up here on the bloody open sea. Aaaagh!' She clutched Bunty's arm so hard that Bunty felt her muscles separate.

But then all hell let loose, and a potentially broken arm was suddenly the least of her worries. With a pitching motion that Bunty felt sure would catapult them all into the sea, the yacht broke free of the confines of the harbour and plunged into open waters, towards the harbour bridge. 'Woooo!' screamed one of the passengers in delight, but Bunty could see that she and Kat were not on their own. Half the tourists were clutching each other or the side of the boat as if their life depended on it. Maybe it did.

Kat screwed up her eyes and refused to look, bleating like a lost sheep whenever they tipped again over a bigger wave, which was about every three seconds. There was a resounding crack, and this time nearly all the passengers screamed.

'That didn't sound right,' said the captain cheerfully. 'John, get up there and have a look, will ya?' John, clearly the most junior of the crew, was strapped into a net which looked about strong enough to hold a kilo of oranges, and was hoisted up the mast. Ten, twenty, thirty feet he went, then suddenly the yacht pitched sideways, John swung out beyond the deck over the grey and unforgiving waves, and Bunty's stomach lurched. 'This is sailing?' she screamed to Kat. 'This is sailing, which Ben loves so much? We're going to die!'

Kat was muttering a prayer under her breath, just at the moment the captain yelled, 'Right, we're bringing the boom over, so you all have to swap sides … now!'

'Christ! We were talking during this bit,' moaned Bunty.

'Duck!' screamed Kat as a swinging tree trunk headed in their direction, while the captain glared at Bunty and yelled 'Other side!'

They'd have had an easier job climbing Rangitoto with the girls, backpack full of David or not. The deck of the boat was now at a seventy degree angle, slopping about with water and what Bunty strongly suspected was vomit. 'Up there?' They were now expected to run at a crouch, uphill, dodging the boom as it flew towards them.

'NOW!' she screamed to Kat, grabbing her friend's hand and hauling her as best she could up the incline. There was no way that Kat's wedges could grip the wooden decking and she pitched forward onto her knees. 'Leave me, I'll swim,' she cried pathetically, but she was still wading on her hands and knees up to the other side, Bunty trying to push her along from behind. It was about the most undignified, and certainly the most terrified, that Bunty had ever been.

Kat dragged herself to her feet and let out a long, shuddering breath. 'I. Hate. You.'

'I'm sorry.' Bunty could quite see why. The side of the yacht where they'd been standing just moments ago was now completely underwater; NZL 40 was practically on its side, zipping across the ocean with John-in-a-net swinging madly over their heads as he proffered a Gallic shrug down to the captain, and the whole process was about to start again.

As calmly as possible, Bunty said, 'Kat, get ready.'

'I didn't tell Simon I love him,' said Kat in a weak voice.

'He knows.' Bunty took Kat's freezing cold hand and forced her into a crouching position. Charlotte would just 'know' too, wouldn't she, if Bunty died out at sea? And her parents. And Graham … and Ben. Ben would never know. 'Come on!' she screamed, dragging Kat as best she could back up the slope which had appeared again in front of them.

'We made it! Better!'

Bunty drew in breath and looked around her. It was almost fun, really. A couple of the tourists had hold of the winches and were winding madly, operating the sail or the boom or … some part of it anyway, and she could almost start to see the appeal, if it weren't all quite so wet. She was drenched to the knees, her bottom soaked too where she'd leaned against the side which had previously been submerged. Kat – she could hardly dare look at Kat – appeared almost naked from the waist down as her white linen trousers turned into tissue paper.

Kat saw it herself. 'Thank God for big knickers!' she hissed, looking as though she intended to beat Bunty to death with them as soon as they were on dry land.

'We're off again,' warned Bunty. She was getting the hang of it now. Given a couple more tries, she might even relax enough to have a go at the winchy thing. Impress Ben. 'Wonder what the winchy-wheel thing is called?'

They hobbled together under the boom, but this time it was worse. With a lunge, the boat side behind them dipped far below the surface, and the deck in front of them seemed almost vertical. They scrabbled on their knees to the other side as if they were on the scree-covered slopes of a mountain. 'Whoops!' called the ever-chirpy captain.

'I'm going to kill him,' said Kat. 'If he doesn't drown us I'm going to kill him.'

'It's not that bad,' said Bunty. 'If you just go a bit sooner … What?'

'What … what the hell's that?'

Bunty followed Kat's wrinkled finger. 'No! Stop the boat. Our bags!'

Their bags – and not just theirs, but the bags of several other passengers and quite a few light jackets and cardigans – had slid to the side of the yacht, gone under as the boat tipped once more, and were now floating out to sea beyond even the reach of John-in-a-net.

'Whoops,' said the captain.

'I'll fucking whoops him,' said Kat murderously, but her words were whipped away by the rising wind, and instead of moving she clung helplessly to Bunty's arm, which was the position in which they endured the next hour and a half.

Someone had fished the nearest items out of the ocean, and to their great elation the mound of soggy offerings included Kat and Bunty's bag. Kat shook out her money and headed for the nearest bar, where the melodic guitar duo were belting out James Taylor numbers.

'I need a drink, or I need to hit somebody,' she said.

'Drink,' agreed Bunty, fishing out her phone. 'We'll laugh about this one day. Do you remember that day in Auckland …'

'Where we nearly died. Tee hee. What fun. Oh God, I'm only joking, Bunty. What's the matter?'

Bunty's eyes filled with tears. She pressed the on-button of her phone again. And Again. 'We might not have died,' she said. 'But my phone has.'

'Oh Bunty,' said Kat, throwing a wet, bedraggled arm around Bunty's shoulders. 'Rum?'

'It has to be,' said Bunty. The phone was dead. Her sailor was gone. Rum was the only fitting drink. 'A large one.'

CHAPTER NINETEEN

Fortunately the two guys on guitar, Mel and Chad, were far more helpful than the Americas Cup crew who seemed intent only on murder. After playing a succession of eighties guitar classics and half the repertoire from Crowded House, they came over to introduce themselves to the most enthusiastic clappers in the room. In fact, the only clappers in the room.

Bunty couldn't understand it. 'I thought we British were the ones who were meant to be reserved,' she called to Kat during a Tom Waits number. 'What's wrong with these miserable buggers?'

'Maybe they're German,' said Kat, which for some reason they both found incredibly hilarious. 'Let's ask them.'

Bunty squinted at her rum. Third, was it? She'd only just remembered that she didn't actually like rum. Couldn't think why. It was actually very nice. 'I'm not asking some complete strangers why Germans don't clap.'

'No,' said Kat, 'the guitar guys. They're coming over. Guitar guys,' she said directly to them. 'We have a question for you.'

'Mel and Chad,' said the guitarist, who also played the keyboard.

'Bunty wants to know,' slurred Kat, 'why we are the only ones clapping.'

'Goes with the territory,' said Chad, with the same easy nonchalance as the crew captain on NZL 40. 'We're used to it. But we have a good time. And you're clearly enjoying it.'

Bunty nodded solemnly, and Kat continued, 'Bunty also wants to know …'

'I don't,' said Bunty, not at all sure what Kat was about to ask.

'You do. Bunty also wants to know where Ben is. Ben with a yacht.'

Mel stroked his chin. 'Hm. Do you have any other information?'

'No. Yes!' Bunty sat up abruptly. 'Yes. Sitting Bull.'

'I only asked …'

'No. The man on the phone said 'Sitting Bull.' Or … sitting something. I didn't hear the rest.'

Mel and Chad looked at each other. 'Ben with a yacht. I'm thinking …'

'Eastport Marina,' said Chad with a nod.

'The Sitting Duck,' finished Mel. 'It's a cafe. A lot of the yachties grab a bite in there.'

'That's it,' said Bunty softly. She'd discovered the Holy Grail. The eating place of yachties. 'The Sitting Duck. Oh, thank you. Thank you!'

'Yes, thank you, guitar guys! Mil and Chud. Thank you. We will clap even more!' said Kat, demonstrating large clapping and slipping off her stool.

Chad grinned. 'We're here every Sunday. Save some for next week.'

'So all we have to do now,' yelled Bunty over a fairly raucous Eagle-Eye Cherry number, 'is get in a cab to Eastport Marina and shout. Shout 'Be-en', and there he'll be! My Ben!'

217

'Sh'perfect,' said Kat solemnly. 'And we'll do better than a cab. Shimon … oops … Shimon will give us a lift. I'll call him.'

'Yes, you call him on your little working phone that didn't drown, while I go and make myself beautiful in the loos.'

'Bunty.' Kat leaned over, glassy eyed, and pawed Bunty's hair. 'You're already beautiful. Silly Graham if he can't see it. Ha. He'll be sorry.'

'He will! He will be sorry. Because I am … beautiful. Like you.'

Bunty staggered off upstairs to the strains of Kat wheedling Simon into cab-driving. This was a great place. She would come here lots when she and Ben lived together, maybe six months here and six months in the UK. They'd be like a celebrity couple, 'dividing their time between' New Zealand and the UK. Between his kids and her kids. Oops. No. Best not go there. Get the houses sorted first, she told herself as she approached the mirror.

Jesus. She looked like a train wreck. Half her hair was flat to her head while the other half – the side that had been in the wind, presumably, stuck out like a cockatoo's crest. Her non-waterproof mascara had slid down her face in the squalls, and there was a definite crusty finish to her jaw line. Dabbing at it, Bunty sucked the end of her finger. Salt. She was a salty sea dog. Or just a dog, she thought with a wince.

After attempting to scrub off the mascara with toilet paper, Bunty accepted that the crested crown of her hair was never going to lie down, so she slopped water across her head and hung upside down under the hair dryer. Her short hair dried in a couple of minutes, and she sashayed back down the stairs to the door, where Kat was now leaning gratefully on Simon.

'Holy crap,' shrieked Kat. 'Did you get an electric shock? I am so going to sue those guys, losing our bags and then sending you into a haz ... haz ... dodgy area all wet.'

'No.' Bunty drew herself up to her full nearly five feet. Might even be five feet with my extra hair height, she thought. 'I like it. It's the Kiwi me. Let's go.'

With as much dignity as two fairly drunk, middle-youth women could muster, Bunty and Kat sauntered out of the bar, blew raspberries at the bobbing NZL 40 before them, and followed Simon to his car.

'Are you sure you want to go to the marina right now?' said Simon, looking from Kat to Bunty with concern and more than a touch of amusement.

'No time like the present,' said Kat.

'The present is ... the present,' agreed Bunty.

Kat nodded. 'It's a gift. That's what the present is. It's a gift.'

'*Carpe diem*. Seize the moment. There's no time like a gift.'

'All right,' said Simon. 'It's your funeral.'

Kat turned to Bunty. 'He's a man. He doesn't understand. But I do.'

'Because you're my friend,' said Bunty, nodding wisely.

They discussed their friendship in fairly circular terms for quite a few minutes. Bunty knew that she should be focussing, working out a plan of action, but somehow it seemed too hard to do. She's far rather reminisce with Kat about their various nights out together, and exchange 'd'ye remembers'. All too soon, however, they pulled up at a dockside.

'Haven't we just been here?' said Bunty, peering into the thickening gloom. 'Bar. Boats. Water. We've gone round in a big circle.'

'Simon, you idiot, we've gone round in a big circle.' Kat opened the car door and peered up at the bar. 'Oh. No. That isn't the bar we were just in. It's the Sitting Duck.'

'Trust me now?' said Simon, killing the engine.

Bunty clambered out, trying to resist the temptation to pull her wet jeans out of her behind in case someone important was watching. He could be here. He could be here, right now. But disappointment swooped down on her. 'It's closed.'

Simon studied the opening hours, which Bunty could barely even see. 'It's more of a cafe than a bar. It opens during the day. Looks like it closed,' he checked his watch, 'an hour ago. Sorry, Bunty.'

Bunty wanted to sink to the floor and wail. It could hardly make any difference to how damp she was. 'So far. So far and he's not here.' A tear trickled down the side of her nose.

She looked out across the marina. It was hopeless. There was jetty after jetty, stretching out for miles across the water's edge, each with dozens of yachts bobbing on either side like beads on a necklace. The sums were so big she couldn't even do them, but there had to a thousand boats here. Two thousand maybe. And most of them appeared to be unoccupied. Empty. Ben-less. The loneliness felt tangible.

It was only as Simon was holding the car door open for Bunty to get back in that she became seized with rage. How dare he not be here? She'd travelled all this way to make her bloody grand gesture and win over the man of her dreams, and he didn't even have the decency to be here waiting for her. 'No,' she said firmly. 'I'm going to find that man and give him a piece of my mind. Mr Bloody Ten Days, messing me about like that and making me really, really want him.'

Because there was the crux of it. His coming and going, his leaving and indifference – they were so incredibly attractive. He was elusive. Glamorous. Hard to pin down. Well, he wasn't going to treat Bunty, former queen of the flirts, like she was some nobody he could pick up and drop whenever he felt like it.

Invigorated, Bunty marched up to the nearest gate to a jetty. No entry. There was an intercom security panel next to her, but when random pressing of the buttons failed to open the gate, she grabbed it with both hands and shook it like a crazed prisoner. So be it. She was a crazed prisoner, trapped in this situation until Ben released her. Or loved her back. 'Hello!' she hollered, rattling as loudly as she could. 'Is Ben there? Hello!'

A woman, well-padded in a fleece and tracksuit, jumped off the back of a small yacht thirty yards away and approached the gate. 'Hi. Forgotten the code?'

'No, I'm looking for someone,' said Bunty, trying to sound and look a lot calmer – and less drunk – than she was. 'Ben.'

'Ben with a yacht,' shouted Kat helpfully from the car.

The woman looked non-plussed, but then Bunty had a brainwave. 'He just got back from England. Ben, with a yacht, and he just went to England.'

'Oh, yeah,' said the woman. 'Ben Maikelekelevesi.'

'Um, probably,' said Bunty. The name sounded long and complicated enough.

'He was telling us about it today in there.' The woman pointed to the Sitting Duck.

'Then he's here? He's here now?'

'On the daily boat, Pier 21. The code's 3421,' added the woman. She waved as she climbed back aboard her boat, and Bunty turned to Kat, hardly able to move.

'You go, girl,' said Kat. 'We'll wait here.'

Pier 21 was several jetties away. What had the woman said? The daily boat. Must be like a hotel for sailors. Though why wouldn't Ben be on his yacht? Of course, he'd never said he lived on it the whole time. He hadn't actually, now she thought about it, said where he did live most of the time. Pier 20. Bunty's heart rose into her throat. The torture of not knowing whether he might be there was almost unbearable, so unbearable she nearly turned back, but Kat was there in the distance waving her on, so she trod carefully onto Pier 21.

Number 3421. The gate swung open before her. 'The daily boat, the daily boat,' she reminded herself, going past *Sunset Girl*, *Paid 4* and *Tarragone*, and several other yachts and boats of varying sizes. None of the smaller ones fitted the bill, and she was just wondering whether to scare someone witless by knocking on the cabin window when she moved into the area out in deeper waters where the bigger yachts were moored. And suddenly there it was, not the daily boat, as she had thought, but the 'Daly' boat, with *Daly Bread* scribed in careful cursive along the mahogany veneer.

There was a light on in the cabin. She leaned down to tap, but in her ear a familiar voice said, 'Bunty. What the hell – the *hell* – are you doing here?'

CHAPTER TWENTY

'Jesus, Graham, you gave me the fright of my life.'

Bunty clutched the side of *Daly Bread* for support, bobbing up and down with it as she stared in horror, then confusion, at her red-faced husband.

'Right,' said Graham, pacing up and down the jetty, half-running to her, stepping back, hardly in control of his own movements. 'I gave you a fright. What kind of fright do you think you gave me? A note? A *note*, Bunty. My wife and my daughter gone. Disappeared to fucking New Zealand. The other side of the world, Bunty. The *world*.'

'Bunty?' Another voice sounded in her ear, behind her again. What was it with these men, lurking around behind her back like some kind of pantomime baddies. 'Bunty, what …? Is that …?'

Bunty took a deep breath and turned around. Ben. He looked utterly adorable, tanned and broad-shouldered, wearing a small boy on his hip as his board shorts flapped gently in the breeze.

'This is him, then, is it?' Graham pranced from one foot to the other. 'I ought to bloody deck you, mate, but seeing as you're holding a kid and what have you … nah, put the kid down. Lemme deck you.'

'Graham, stop! Ben, this is … hi.'

Oh God, this couldn't be happening. Bunty covered her face with her hands. There was Ben doing his adoring father impression, looking so solid and dependable and downright bloody huggable, and then … Graham. Graham, livid and scarlet and running around in little half-circles as if he didn't know what to do, or who to punch, first. And talking about decking someone like he'd ever smacked another human being in his life.

Bunty half-turned her back on Graham in the hope that he wouldn't be able to hear her. 'Ben, I … I needed to see you, so I came … to see you,' she whispered hoarsely.

'You came all the way here … just to see me? Far out!' Ben reached over and put the little boy down on the deck. 'Go down in the cabin, Jarred, I'll be down soon,' he said to his son. The boy looked at Bunty with his father's black eyes and then scampered down the steps. Pretty soon his nose was pressed against the cabin window in readiness for the show.

Ben turned back to Bunty. 'That's incredible, Bunty, but … why?'

'Why?' shouted Graham. 'Why do you think, you daft bastard? Cos she wants some sailing lessons? Because she's in love with you. Not me, her poor bloody husband. You!'

He hopped around some more, strangely enough not taking the opportunity that had now presented itself to 'deck' Ben as he'd hitherto been desperate to do, but still unable to keep his movements to himself.

'Husband?' said Ben, nodding.

'Ex,' said Bunty, hardly able to speak. 'Soon to be ex.'

'When you left me for him,' thundered Graham.

'No, no, when you left me for Verity Reynolds.'

'Verity Reynolds? I'm not bloody leaving you for Verity Reyolds!'

'But … then …'

Bunty swallowed down the enormous lump in her throat, horribly confused. She didn't know which part of Graham's statement to address first. Was he leaving her but for someone else? Was he leaving her anyway and Verity Reynolds was just the lucky bonus? Did he admit that he had been seeing a pert-bottomed blonde called Verity Reynolds? He didn't seem surprised about the name, just that Bunty might think he was leaving for her. Leaving. He was leaving her, wasn't he?

'You are leaving me, though, aren't you?'

Graham gave her a look so pained, so filthy, so full of hate that Bunty felt she would spear herself on it on the hour, every hour, for the rest of her life.

'I am now,' he said quietly.

After one last little jig of frustration, of anguish, he turned on his heel and walked away down the jetty.

Bunty watched him, aghast. He was leaving her. Graham was actually leaving her. And … she'd got it wrong. He hadn't wanted to replace her with a new pneumatic blonde model, but she'd forced him into it now. And Ben …

'Oh God, Ben,' she said, knowing that if she turned around to him now Graham would see, would know somehow through the cold prickle of the skin on his shoulders.

Ben put a hand on her shoulder, and she felt the old rush of warmth slide over her, but suddenly stop.

'Go after him,' he said softly.

'But I want you,' she said balefully. Even as the words came out of her mouth and their eyes met soulfully, she realised it wasn't really true. Some part of her wanted him, for sure. The part that needed attention and big gestures. The part that lived inside her head, in her imagination.

Ben let out a small, cold laugh. 'Why?'

'I …'

'I've been a self-absorbed prick. I've stood you up. I've let you down. I've lied about myself. But then it looks like I wasn't the only one.'

'You've … what lies?' The floor beneath Bunty's feet rocked and she was sure it was neither the water nor the rum making it move. Lies? 'What lies, Ben?'

Ben coughed in a way that suggested, ominously, that he was about to start on a list. 'Well, the yacht. Not mine, of course. Belongs to the Daly brothers. I just crew it for them.'

'But you were living it on it.'

Ben shook his head. 'Do you think I could get it to and from England, on my own, in that short a time? I'd be in the world records. Nah, I was staying with Cilla.'

It was Bunty's turn to shake her head. 'Cilla? Your … wife?'

'Cilla of the Croesus Club. Priscilla, to you. She's an old mate from when I was in London on my OE, years ago. She needed men for her dating thing, so I offered to stand in.'

More rocking. 'Priscilla's … Cilla's a friend?'

'With benefits,' said Ben with a flash in his eyes.

'Oh … my … God.'

Bunty breathed in, lights starting to flash around the edges of her eyes as if she were coming down with a migraine, which she'd never had in her life. But she'd never before been presented with a lying bastard who'd been nothing he promised to be. Never. Except …

She remembered something. 'So you're not married? These aren't your kids? Did you steal them or something?'

For the first time Ben's face softened, and she saw something of the old Ben, the sweet and simple Ben that she'd been – God, it hurt to even think of it – dating.

'No, I really was married. Kids are really mine. That's why I was in England, catching up with Cilla. My wife left me. For my best friend.'

It was hard to know what to say. Perhaps because you're a lying shit, she was tempted to say. But who knew the truth really? She didn't exactly have a clean record herself, did she?

'I'm sorry,' she said simply.

'Yeah, well, it won't last. She said she loved him and everything, and chucked me out.' Ben was talking at a pace now, his voice sharp and edgy as she'd never heard it before. 'That's why I went away. But she didn't move him in, so she can't really love him, can she?'

I don't know, Bunty thought. I don't really know what love is any more, but, 'Why not?' she said.

Ben laughed again, that harsh, 'are-you-an-idiot' laugh that he'd issued before. 'Because then she'd want to see him all the time, wouldn't she? Christ, if I met someone I really liked I'd want to be with them twenty-four seven.'

She couldn't have sobered up more quickly if he'd hung her in the water over the dockside by her hair. Twenty-four seven.

Not every couple of weeks, on a ten-day turnaround if she was lucky. She recognised the tone of his voice too. '

You're still in love with her.'

Ben nodded. 'I've come back to try to persuade her to change her mind. She says … she says we can give it a go. Not working out quite so well with lover boy.' That bitter laugh again. 'Don't get me wrong, though. You are lovely, Bunty. A great person.'

'Yep, that's me,' said Bunty. 'Really great. Salt of the earth. Dating when I'm still married. Being blown away by someone I hardly know, someone who seems … Shit!'

For the first time it hit her. That was why she'd liked him. Loved him even. That was why she'd yearned for him, followed him across the world, recognised him. Adam. He was the new Adam. The anti-Graham. Unavailable, unassailable, and frankly downright bloody horrible on occasions.

Any anger she'd been about to express (and there'd been a bit – like, Was I a game? I hear Kiwis like their sport, and, Jesus, you *were* just a slut with a shag bag while I was trying to turn you into Mr fucking Rochester!) disappeared like air from a pricked balloon. She was no better than he was. And he no worse than she. They'd both just been running away, chasing down a dream. It had all been in her head. Her own *Brief Encounter* moment, without any of the emotion other than a bit of a frisson, an edge of excitement.

When she raised her head to tell him she was genuinely sorry, Ben was looking at her, an amused smile at the corner of his lips.

'I can't believe you, though,' he said after a moment.

'What?' There was quite a lot not to believe; Bunty could see that.

'Getting on a plane and coming all the way out here just to see me. I never even gave you my number, for Chrissakes.'

Hmm, that was true. How desperate did that make her sound? It was extra nice of him to point that out. Bastard.

'Well, don't take it personally,' said Bunty quickly. 'I was just bored.'

Double bastard. Ben bastard and Adam bastard, all rolled up in one.

It was time to go. Ben's son seemed to agree, as he was now squashing his face against the glass and smearing snot down it. Bunty pointed to him.

'Christ, the Daly brothers will kill me. They don't even know I'm having the kids over here.'

Ben started towards the yacht, then turned around with a quirk of an eyebrow that would have had Bunty stripping, or possibly spontaneously combusting, just a few weeks before now. 'I'll text you, and then you'll have my number, Crazy Lady.'

'Too late, Ad ... Ben,' said Bunty. 'My phone died. And I don't want your number anyway.'

This was just the moment, she reflected as she walked away, that Ben would be especially interested in her. It was his loss.

But just what, she wondered, would her loss be.

'Graham!' she shouted. 'Wait!'

He was sandwiched between Kat and Simon, who had both linked arms with him as if he were a convict. 'I couldn't let him drive,' said Simon, struggling to hold Graham down as Bunty approached. 'He's just so incensed he'd drive Cally's car off the wharf.'

'Don't fucking talk about me like I'm not fucking here!' Graham wriggled with more athleticism than Bunty would have ever imagined he possessed, and she could instantly see just how fit he had become.

'Graham! Graham, calm down. We need to talk.'

'Oh!' he roared. 'You want to talk now, do you? After your piece of ... trouser's dumped you because you're too much trouble? Not weeks ago when I wanted to talk. Well, I DON'T FEEL LIKE TALKING!'

'Is he on something?' asked Kat, tightening her grip.

'You're doing it again! NO, I AM NOT ON SOMETHING. NOT EVEN MY WIFE. IN FACT, I AM NEVER ON MY BLOODY WIFE THESE DAYS.'

'And why's that?' said Bunty, fed up with shag bags and over-sexed men. 'You've been having an affair! You're getting all you want away from home. Don't think I don't know the signs, Graham – losing weight, getting fit, whitening your teeth, for God's sake, your bloody teeth! And football matches that don't exist and Verity Reynolds, and you had a vasectomy, Graham, a vasectomy so I couldn't have any more children, without even asking me.'

Graham was bucking like a steer in Simon and Kat's grip, looking distinctly like he was either having a fit, or he needed to be Tazered.

'I wasn't having an affair, you suspicious cow, I was trying to be interesting. Interesting! For you. I was making a great big bloody gesture like those stupid men on your endless fucking television programmes. You were so bored! *Bored*! I could see it in your face every time I came home.'

'But Verity Reynolds? I ... I *was* bored, it's true.' Bunty looked at her poor wretch of a husband, tears of rage and Lord only knew what else coursing down his cheeks.

'Well, I've got to tell you,' screamed Graham, 'you're not so bloody fascinating yourself these days.'

At which point, Kat's eyes grew very round, Simon dropped Graham's arm, and Bunty staggered backwards. His words hurt her more than anything Ben could ever have said or done, because deep in her heart she knew it was true, and everyone knew that the truth hurt. All this time, she – and not just Bunty, but everyone around her – had considered Graham to be the lucky one, while she had merely 'settled' for someone dependable. Someone who wasn't Adam. But what if it was the other way round. What if she'd been the lucky one? And what if now, through her own stupidity, her luck had just run out?

Graham shook himself free of Kat and Simon. He seemed calmer now, even, for a moment, as though he might be about to apologise, but then he walked over to Cally's car, which was possibly stolen, and reached for his bag on the back seat.

He strode up to Bunty with a vigour she hadn't seen in many years.

'There,' he said bitterly, thrusting something into her hand. 'There's your bloody grand gesture. I was crap anyway. Didn't work any way you look at it.'

Bunty stared after the car. What did he mean, he was crap anyway? Chasing her across the world – that was a pretty big sacrifice for a proud man to make – was a grand gesture indeed. But then she realised he'd been talking about the object in her hand, and she stared at it, hardly able to think any more.

'It's a video tape,' she told Kat.

'Your wedding?'

Bunty shook her head. 'I've never seen it before.' She read the label with no comprehension. 'Graham. *On the Sofa.*'

'Oh my good God, it's something really perverted,' said Kat.

But Bunty knew that Graham would never humiliate her like that. He'd always watched out for her feelings, saved her embarrassment. Saved her even from embarrassing herself – until now. 'Watch it with me,' she said.

CHAPTER TWENTY-ONE

It took nearly four months for the damage to be undone, which was coincidentally about the amount of time it had taken to create it all. Kat had a theory that it was always the case, a sort of relationship quid pro quo system. 'It's like, 'Create one bad month and I'll give you one for free',' she said over drinks in early February, when she was finally back, leaving behind the New Zealand summer.

Bunty sighed. 'Well, I did a very good job of it. I deserve every bit of penance, I suppose.'

'It wasn't all your fault,' said Kat, watching Dan's behind through the window as he dropped some piping off in Bunty's garage. 'Graham always was pretty boring, let's face it. Who could possibly have imagined what he was up to?'

Who indeed? Certainly not Bunty, who had sat on Cally's sofa with her hand on her chest, roughly where her heart was bleeding, and her mouth open in wonderment as Pearl and Finn appeared on the TV screen. 'On the sofa? Oh my life.'

Pearl was introducing a new section: 'Finance with Farradays'. Suddenly, shatteringly, there was Graham, gleaming of tooth and looking, well, almost handsome in his current skinny Shrekky way, a nice open neck shirt under his new dark-blue suit jacket, stammering only slightly over his beginnings but picking up speed and credibility as he began to discuss stakeholder pensions for the benefit of the viewers.

'He's met Pearl and Finn,' whispered Bunty.

'Are those two shagging?' Kat squinted at the screen. 'They've got to be shagging, surely? They're so chummy and giggly.'

'Kat, wrong moment,' warned Cally, evidently still feeling slightly guilty for having told Graham what Kat had passed on to her – that they'd gone to Eastport Marina to find someone called Ben.

Bunty watched her husband – her almost-handsome, do-anything-for-her husband – facing all his fears at once and talking to the camera, and felt tears sting her eyes. He couldn't possibly have done more to combat his biggest fear of all – losing her. But it was too late.

Cally handed her a tissue. 'He told us – well, ranted – all about it. How he'd thought you might want sex with him if you didn't think it would lead to more kids. How he'd realised how fed up you were and decided to reinvent himself just to keep you happy. He even thought about what you liked best, which is apparently these two,' she jerked a finger at the TV, 'and not me and Kat, which upset me a bit, I have to say.'

'Anyway,' piped up Pete from the kitchen where he was on calming-cups-of-tea duty, 'his company said they wanted volunteers for this job, and he and some other bloke went up for it.'

'Ryan!' squeaked Kat. 'Christ, you can see why Graham got the gig. Anyone's got to be better than Ryan.'

'Watch it,' said Bunty.

235

'Apparently the other guy's quite good too, according to Graham,' said Pete, handing Bunty a mug. 'They had media training and everything with some consultant.'

Bunty and Kat stared at each other. 'Verity Reynolds!' they said together. 'I thought he was having an affair with her,' groaned Bunty.

Pete shook his head. 'Don't think so. Although he did say –'

'Pete,' Cally said in a warning voice again. Bunty looked sideways at her. Since when was she so careful about what everyone said?

'What? I want to know.'

Cally rubbed her arm. 'He did say he'd had the chance to … you know … with Verity Reynolds, and he was very sorry he'd turned it down seeing as you were shagging everyone in town.'

'But I wasn't! I was trying … but I wasn't!'

To think she'd nearly gotten down to it with Ben. Bloody horrible Ben. Thank God it had never happened. But Graham, funny Graham with his sticky-out ears, nodding so knowledgeably at Finn's fatuous questions, had nearly had someone else. Had, in fact, been wanted by someone else. He suddenly looked doubly attractive in Bunty's eyes.

'Why didn't you stop me?' she wailed at Cally. 'You wanted to, I know. All that stuff about supporting me and not understanding me. You don't even like Graham.'

'No, but I know you do, Bun-hun, and that's enough for me.' Cally rolled her eyes at Pete. 'Anyway, don't blame me, I didn't know anything about it until you were practically on the doorstep. Blame Kat.'

'That's right,' said Bunty, rounding on her other friend. 'You. You encouraged me all along. It's your fault. I wouldn't have done any of this if it weren't for you.'

Kat shrugged, her round eyes pained. 'I thought you were enjoying yourself. You looked like you were having fun. I hadn't seen you that energised in ages.'

'Oh. So it's true, then. I am boring.' Bunty slumped back into the sofa cushions, tears threatening again.

'No,' said Kat firmly. 'Not boring. Bored. You were just bored.'

She had a point. Even when Charlotte padded into the room in her pyjamas saying, 'Where's Dad? Why's he on telly?' and Bunty gathered her up against her side, planning on never letting her go, Bunty realised that it wasn't enough. Charlotte, the house, the tennis club, archery, even inventing perfect men – it wasn't enough. She needed more. Something real and enveloping, warm and fulfilling, like … She thought instantly of the perfect person.

'Can I borrow your phone?' she said to Kat, checking the clock on the kitchen wall. 'It's midnight here, so it'll be what in the UK?'

'About midday,' said Cally.

So she wouldn't be waking anyone up. She wrote her message, found the number on Kat's contact list, and pressed send: 'I need to talk to you. I'll be home in a few days, can I contact you then? Oh. This is Bunty not Kat.'

Moments later the answer came back: 'Sure babes'. And Bunty had smiled as she began to make her plans to a degree that would have made Graham proud.

They had come home to find the place vacant. Even the house had an injured air to it.

'Where's Dad?'

Charlotte wandered from room looking for him, with Bunty sensing the rising desperation in her search. She felt rather the same herself. All this time she'd imagined that it was she, Bunty, who was the cornerstone of the home, but it did feel treacherously empty without Graham, without any prospect of him coming through the door and annoying the bejasus out of her by dropping his briefcase on the sofa and eating his leftover sandwiches before dinner. Not that he did that any more. He didn't do anything any more.

He'd left her a note. Touché, thought Bunty, swallowing hard as she picked up the one remaining sheet of Basildon Bond that had clung to the redundant writing pad. In a certain light she could still see the imprint of her own writing, informing him she was taking their daughter and leaving.

'Bunty and Charlotte,' it said. 'I've just moved out to give you some space while we sort things out. I'll be in touch.'

Charlotte read it over Bunty's shoulder. 'Well, that's great. That's really great. Well done, Mum. I don't know what was going on but, like, totally well done.' And she gulped down a shuddering sigh.

'Oh, sweetheart,' said Bunty, kissing her daughter's forehead. It occurred to her that pretty soon she'd have to reach up to do that. Or she could start a new trend for kissing kids on the chin. 'It's not that bad. Don't go getting all emo on me.'

'Emo?' Charlotte reeled around, her eyes flashing dangerously. 'I'm not blimmin' emo! Am I wallowing in my own dark abyss? No! I don't think so. I'm just flippin' sad, Mum. My dad has moved out. And it's all your fault.'

She stomped off to empty out her suitcase, leaving Bunty in an empty room, empty-hearted. Sighing, Bunty wondered through to the kitchen. Maybe a glass of wine would help. She'd just poured a puddle into the bottom of the glass when she became aware that someone was watching her. There someone on in the garden. Definitely – she could sense it. 'Graham …? Oh shit,' she called. Grabbing the phone so that she could call the police if she found a crazed murderer on her back doorstep, she willed herself to turn around.

They weren't in the garden at all, but in Mary's garden, peering over the fence – her beautiful denim-blue fence, both pairs of eyes accusing, but tinged with sadness. Steeling herself, Bunty opened the back door and headed off down the garden.

'You're back then,' said Graham.

'What have you been up to, love?' said Mary.

Mallory's head popped up next to Mary's, and Bunty's heart sank. How much had he told them? 'Well, I for one think it's grand to see you again, young Bunty.' And he gave her a broad, conspiratorial wink.

'Thank you, Mallory. Yes, I'm back. What are you doing over there?'

Graham's head flipped from side to side, so that for a moment it looked oddly like an executive toy, ears flapping to and fro. 'I said in the note. I've moved out to give us some space.'

'To Mary's?'

'It's a mutually beneficial arrangement,' said Graham huffily. 'Mary gets an income and I get affordable, convenient accommodation.'

Bunty's eyes filled with tears. 'Oh, Graham.' What a love. It was such a stupidly Graham-type answer – none of the underlying emotional stresses and all of the money issues. He was perfect for Farradays *On the Sofa*. Perfect in many ways. Even for her. Especially for her. 'I'm sorry. I'm so sorry. Could we …?'

She'd have liked a private discussion without Mary and Mallory flanking him like Bill and Ben round Little Weed, but Graham cleared his throat, pre-announcement. 'Not ready for that yet, if you don't mind. Now, Mallory and I have rigged up this step-ladder arrangement,' he said, indicating the makeshift stairs running up to the top of the fence and then down the other side, 'so Charlotte can come and visit, or, you know, when I'm ready, I can perhaps come over to maybe see … her.'

'Of course,' said Bunty softly. 'I ... Mallory, Mary, could you …? Oh, sod it. I do love you, you know, Graham.'

Graham stared at her balefully, his ears turning pink, and Mallory discreetly pulled Mary away. 'Right. Well, that's a bit of credit in the bank, I suppose,' he said gruffly. 'We're …. having tea in a minute. Charlotte might want to come over.'

'Right. Yes. I'll go and tell her.'

240

She made it up the path and inside to inform Charlotte of the new arrangements, and back out to the back door to wave her off, before the tears began in earnest. What was the point of it all, she wondered as she sobbed into her wine, sitting on the floor of the kitchen where she wouldn't be seen through the window. What was the bloody point?

And then she remembered her plan, and someone who was waiting for a call. 'A plan, Dan, the drainage man,' she said with intermittent sniffs, pulling the phone down from the worktop.

'Dan, hi, it's Bunty. Is this too late?'

Dan sounded genuinely pleased to hear from her. 'Hi! Thank God! I've been bursting with curiosity as to what you wanted to talk to me about. I'm guessing it's not Flinders raising his mangy head again?'

'No, it's not.'

'You can imagine what I've been thinking,' said Dan with an earthy chuckle.

'What everyone else will be thinking, I expect. But I don't want to have an affair with you. Oddly enough.' Bunty summoned up her courage. 'It's not … It's nothing like that.'

Dan paused, then said, 'That's good, if I'm honest, because, well, you're my mate, aren't you? Wouldn't want all that crap getting in the way.'

'Exactly! Oh, Dan, thank God you said that. Because I've been getting a lot of things wrong and I don't exactly trust my judgement any more, but I thought we were mates, and I hoped we might be … sort of better mates. Because you know how you've got really big hands and mine are little and I can get in small spaces …'

Dan laughed. 'Now you're totally doing my head in.'

'No, I mean … Look, Dan, I need a job. Could I be your apprentice?' There. She'd said it. Finally!

She could almost hear Dan grinning down the phone. 'Who am I, Donald Trump?'

'No, you're Dan, Dan the drainage man. And I could be Bun, Bun the hands down the … yeah, well maybe that won't work. But we could. We'd work well together, wouldn't we? You don't have to pay me much.'

'You're on,' said Dan with barely a pause for thought. 'I've been rushed off my feet and planning to take someone on anyway. Can't think of anyone better. You're not going to be all difficult and want school hours and no weekend work, and that kind of stuff, are you?'

'Yes.'

'Oh, all right then. I'll pick you up tomorrow at nine! Yay!'

If she'd not been so miserable, Bunty would have cheered. Even so, she managed a very large smile and a bottoms-up on her wine glass, and was actually managing a small victory dance round the living room when Charlotte got back. 'Are you all right? We had pie. Do I have to go to school tomorrow? I think I'm jet-lagged.'

'I've got a job!'

Charlotte stopped dead in her tracks. 'You? What the … So are you and Dad getting a di … a divorce?'

'No! God, no, I don't think so. Anyway, I really, really hope not. I love your dad. And I love you. No, I'm going to work with Dan, in drains, near fences. It's just for me. Just to keep me busy and having fun.'

Charlotte, mollified, stared at her from under her fringe. 'Mother,' she pronounced, 'you have a seriously weird idea of fun.'

But it was fun. Tremendous fun. And half of the joy was that being so unlady-like and bogged down in mire and filth, nobody in their right minds could think that she and Dan were an item. They were work mates, good and proper; he taught her the trade, she made the tea.

CHAPTER TWENTY-TWO

The studio itself was a complete let-down. What Bunty had always imagined was actually someone's cosy living room with odd acres of space surrounding it turned out to be an aircraft hanger with a couple of sofas in one corner.

Pearl and Finn, however, were even more magnificent in the flesh, with the same easy banter that was so evident on the screen, and which Bunty now shared with Dan. She listened, bemused and bedazzled, as Pearl listed her IVF treatments to her while discussing Charlotte, as cameras whirled by and one of the men behind a monitor said, 'In ten.'

'Yes, so after the whole turkey-baster thing wasn't going to work, we decided in for a penny, in for a pound, and I booked in with the top gynaecological person in Harley Street, but could I find a woman? No …'

'Five, four …' said monitor man, holding up three fingers, then two.

'… and I really don't want a strange man staring up my crotch and …'

One finger. They were on.

Pearl: Welcome back, everybody. We're here on the sofa today with our brand new feature, 'Drains for Dames.' We've got Dan, Dan the Drainage Man – give the ladies a wave, Dan.

Finn: He's very handy with a plunger, ladies.

Pearl: Now, Finn! And with him, to demonstrate that we women can sort out our own plumbing … Finn! … is Dan's lovely assistant, Bunty McKenna. And Bunty, you're really his assistant, aren't you?

Bunty: (*grinning sheepishly*) Actually I'm his apprentice, so it's all set up through the Enterprise Agency, and I go to college on day release to learn the ropes properly.

Dan: I keep telling her it's pipes, not ropes.

Finn: Oh. Like to handle the ropes, do you, Bunty?

Bunty: I have to handle all sorts in my job, Finn.

Pearl: Now, while Finn stops giggling … Finn … we're going over to Dan's Drains corner where we're going to learn … What is it today, Dan?

Dan: Today, Pearl, we're going to clear out a U-Bend.

Finn: Do you do U-bends too, Bunty? Oh … sorry … (*folds up with laughter*)

Pearl: We were just talking about U-bends off camera, weren't we, Bunty? Okay, show me what to do.

Bunty: Well, the first thing to do, ladies, is to find your stopcock. Finn! You need to turn off your water.

Pearl: (*leaving them demonstrating*) We'll be back to see how Dan and Bunty are getting on later in the show. And now, back to the sofa. Don't forget that tomorrow we've got Ryan from Farradays Finance for those pension tips. Join us after the break.

As the adverts ran, Pearl grinned her familiar toothsome smile at the pair of them. 'Dan and Bunty, you're naturals. I think you're going to go down a storm.'

'Don't you mean a storm drain?' chipped in Finn.

'Finn …' they said in unison.

Bunty beamed. It was a dream come true – literally, in some respects, and in other ways, a dream that she'd never even known she had. There was only one thing left.

CHAPTER TWENTY-THREE

Surprisingly, even Graham got used to the idea after the fourth or fifth sighting of Dan's van had started to cause suspicion. 'You sure there's nothing going on there?' he asked over the fence, one Saturday, several weeks later.

'There's nothing going on anywhere, with anyone,' said Bunty firmly. 'Just working. Does it make me a bit more interesting?'

Graham stared at her, his ears turning pink. 'You have a seriously weird idea of interesting.'

Must be spending too much time with Charlotte, mused Bunty. Great. 'You can talk,' she ventured a little cheekily. 'Mr I-love-things-on-spreadsheets.'

'I love things on bed sheets as well,' said Graham, 'but the financial ones were the only things I could get into for quite a while. I'm hoping that's going to change. Soon.'

'What does … oh, Graham. What does that mean?' Bunty didn't really want to know, but she had to ask. His new-found TV career and honed physique could probably get him laid at the drop of a Personal Equity Plan.

'Just … you know. I've joined one of those dating things. Thought you should know. Mypeople.com, number 45620.'

'You're …' Bunty started to cry. 'You're really moving on?'

Graham took hold of her hand across the fence to stop her crying. 'Well, I can't stay here for ever. The sex is driving me mad.'

'You … you pig!' Bunty wrenched her hand away. 'You're having sex already?'

'Not me. Them,' said Graham, nodding back towards the house. 'Mary and Mallory. It's awful. And sort of amazing. I hope we're still at it like that in our seventies.'

And with a quick peck of her hand, he ducked below the fence line and disappeared.

Bunty stared at her hand for a very long time, a maelstrom of fear and elation swirling beneath her breastbone. Hang on, she thought. He'd been very specific about that dating site. She ran inside at breakneck speed and turned on the computer.

'Come on, come on … There. Mypeople. Yes, I'll pay. Credit card details. Yes, yes, oh bloody hurry up! Yes! Number … what did he say … 45620.'

And suddenly she started to laugh and cry, both at the same time, much to the consternation of Charlotte who was watching something terrible on MTV. 'Are you all right? Have you see this woman's outfit? Can I have ten quid, I'm going to the movies with Saffron tomorrow night.'

Bunty laughed louder. 'Have twenty. Stay out for ages. I'll be out anyway, I think.'

Charlotte shot upright. 'Who with? Not like a … a date?'

'Yes,' said Bunty. 'With this man here. I think you'll like him.'

She and Charlotte read the advert together.

'Totally bloody boring accounts person, looks like Shrek, never been in band or sailed boats or done anything remotely interesting other than marry a fabulous woman and have a marvellous daughter.'

'WLTM short dark woman who looks and thinks like a pantomime Peter Pan, works in drainpipes, preferably with a marvellous daughter. Looking for a date for Valentine's night.'

'All right,' said Charlotte, 'I'll let you.'

'Thanks,' said Bunty. And together they worked out how to send Graham a mighty big smile.

From: admin@croesusclub.com
To: Unnamed recipient – all clients.
To whom it may concern,
Please be aware that the Croesus Club referrals agency will cease to operate as of this Friday, 17 February. The sister agency, Croesus Club NZ, will begin on Monday 20 February, as I am going to join my new partner, Ben, that weekend.

All outstanding monies will be deducted from your credit cards forthwith.

It's been lovely working with you,
Priscilla.

From: buntymckenna@ntmworld.com
To: admin@croesusclub.com
Cilla, you poor bugger. Good luck with that!
Bunty, Graham and Charlotte x

The end

For more about the author and her books, go to

www.jillmarshallwriting.com